'Leg me up,' I hissed as the footsteps headed back the other way. He did, and I was over the wall in a flash. The skip was one of the plastic ʼnd – more like a giant green treasure chest on ˈeels than the open-topped metal buckets ˈders use. I hid behind it till the shop lights aˈˈmed. Then I opened the lid.

ˈˈe was in a white bag with some jigsaws, nˈ ˈ the top. It took me less than twenty seconds ˈ ˈull him out, leap onto a dustbin and go.

'Joel,' Kenny panted, as we hit the park, run-ˈˈg. 'This is totally, totally uncool. What're you ˈnna do with a teddy bear?' He tried to punch ˈ I whisked the bear back.

'Draw him,' I said . . .

ˈut Joel has no idea how much trouble Horace the teddy bear he has just nicked – is going to ˈuse him . . .

www.**kidsatrandomhouse**.co.uk

HORACE

CHRIS d'LACEY

A teddy bear story

CORGI YEARLING BOOKS

HORACE
A CORGI YEARLING BOOK 0440 86445 3

First publication in Great Britain

Corgi Yearling edition published 2004

1 3 5 7 9 10 8 6 4 2

Papers used by Random House Children's Books are natural,
recyclable products made from wood grown in sustainable forests.
The manufacturing processes conform to the environmental
regulations of the country of origin.

Set in 12/15 pt Palatino by
Palimpsest Book Production Limited, Polmont, Stirlingshire

Corgi Yearling Books are published by
Random House Children's Books,
61–63 Uxbridge Road, London W5 5SA,
a division of The Random House Group Ltd,
in Australia by Random House Australia (Pty) Ltd,
20 Alfred Street, Milsons Point, Sydney, NSW 2061, Australia,
in New Zealand by Random House New Zealand Ltd,
18 Poland Road, Glenfield, Auckland 10, New Zealand,
and in South Africa by Random House (Pty) Ltd,
Endulini, 5A Jubilee Road, Parktown 2193, South Africa

THE RANDOM HOUSE GROUP Limited Reg. No. 954009
www.**kids**at**randomhouse**.co.uk

A CIP catalogue record for this book is available from the British Library.

Printed and bound in Great Britain by
CPI Antony Rowe, Eastbourne

for Ptery

With grateful thanks to:
Gurdeep & Channi, Charnjit & Surinderpal
Colin Brooks for being such a star
Frank Webster at House of Bruin
Bead Roberts, who knows about bears and their eyes,
and Fred (50p) for being there.

CHAPTER ONE

On the day I found Horace, I was looking for a birthday present for my mum. She likes thimbles. She's collected them since she was a girl. She keeps them in trays like miniature beehives, stacked three deep underneath her bed. When her birthday comes around, she's easy to please. All you have to do is buy her a thimble. If you can hunt one down, that is.

It's become a competition in our family now: who can find the best thimble soonest. That year, I was trailing, badly. Dad had bought a set of four off the internet (painted with images from *The Wind in the Willows*); Erin, my younger sister, had found one sprouting ceramic purple flowers; and Maddie, the eldest of the three of us, had been crowing that hers had 'Chinese dragons' and was going to knock spots off everyone else's.

So that just left me. I'd been round all the usual places – junk shops, rummage sales, that sort of thing – but they'd turned up nothing and I was getting pretty desperate. Then one Friday after school I had a brainwave. Turning to my best mate, Kenny, I said, 'That charity shop. The one on Dobbs Road. We haven't looked there. Come on, it's not far.'

Kenny groaned and buried his face in his bag. Thimble season really tees him off.

So I dangled him a carrot that never fails. 'You can come for tea afterwards if you want to,' I told him, casually adding, 'Maddie's going riding.' Kenny has a major crush on my sister. He thinks she looks 'cute' in her jodhpurs and hat. It took him less than a second to decide.

'Let's cut through the park. That's quickest,' he said.

So we made it to the shop at about quarter to four. It was one of those neat-looking charity places. Tastefully decorated. Maroon and blue. Big yellow sunflowers on the windows and walls. While Kenny drifted off to have a look at some sports gear, I turned to the shelves of bric-a-brac and hunted. There were loads of ornaments and trinkets and incense. But, annoyingly, not a single thimble.

I was just about to call Kenny over and go, when an old woman at the counter eyed me up. She was plump and grey and had short, bowed legs. When she spoke, she didn't take her hands off the counter. 'Can I help you, dear? We're shutting at four.'

'Do you have any thimbles?' I asked.

Clutching her necklace as though it were a safety chain, she turned to a curtained room behind her. 'Doris, there's a boy here asking for thimbles.'

The curtain swished aside. A younger woman in a *Save the Whale* sweatshirt stepped out. She had some shirts slung loosely over her shoulder and in the crook of one arm she was cradling a straw-coloured, grumpy-looking teddy bear. 'I'm sorry, I sold the only thimble we had last week. Lovely design. Chinese dragons. Young girl bought it for her mum.'

Maddie. I winced.

'We've had some donations today,' she went on, repositioning the bear to fit him to her hip, 'but I haven't had time to go through it all yet.'

Before I could ask how long that would take, Kenny breezed up in a football shirt. The idiot was wearing it over his fleece. It was bright red and clashed with his yellow school tie. 'England strip. Last season's. Monster!' He dug in his pocket and flashed a pound coin. The old dear lifted a hand off the counter. I thought for one moment she might topple over, but she swooped on Kenny's money like a wizened bird of prey. She wobbled to the till and clocked up the sale.

'D'you get one?' he asked, meaning the thimble.

I shook my head. He groaned in disappointment. Mum's birthday was just a few days away now and he knew we'd be in for some heavy-duty searching if we didn't find something soon. But my interest in the hunt had waned for the moment. I couldn't stop staring at that teddy bear.

'Beautiful, isn't he?' Doris said, turning his head so he stared back at me. He had shiny glass eyes, round and orange. The left one was loose and hung down slightly, giving him a sort of far-away look. His nose was a faded leather patch, and his sulky black mouth just three lines of stitching. What really stood out about him, though, were his ears. They resembled a couple of radar dishes. A small elephant would have been proud of them. I wouldn't have called him 'beautiful' exactly. 'Interesting', that's what I would have said. He looked like a bear who'd seen a lot of things.

'How much is he?'

'Eh?' said Kenny.

The old dear cackled. 'You don't want that.'

Doris bounced the teddy bear on her hip, rounding his cupped ears as she spoke. 'Even if he did, he's not for sale. This old boy's about to go into the skip.'

'Why?' I asked, and pulled my face into a frown.

'Who cares?' said Kenny.

I did. I kind of liked the 'old boy'. He had a brilliant profile. I wanted to draw him. Art was my favourite subject at school.

'Regulations,' said Doris, sitting him on the counter. He had heavy, jointed legs and sat up easily. 'We're not allowed to sell on cuddly toys unless they have a European Community safety label. This chap was made well before those laws were introduced. He's probably older than me.'

'Seventy?' gasped Kenny.

'I'm fifty-eight, thank you.' She gave him a withering look.

'If you're going to chuck him out, can't I take him?' I said. 'I'll make a donation. How much would he be if you *could* sell him?'

The old dear dangerously waved a hand. 'Ooh, about fifty pence for that old bag of stuffing, I should think.'

I fished one out of my pocket. 'OK.'

Kenny's eyes nearly popped. 'Joel? What're you doing?'

Doris smiled, but shook her head. 'No. I really can't sell him. Once he's in our care, he's legally our responsibility. If I gave him to you and a young child choked on one of these eyes, we'd be liable. It's a terrible shame to throw him out, I know. But that's the rule, I'm afraid.'

The clock ticked on to four. A cuckoo leaped

out, making Kenny jump. Doris waved the bear's paw. 'We have to cash up and close now. Sorry.'

Cash. I twiddled the coin in my fingers. 'I want to make a donation, anyway.' I dropped the fifty pence into a collecting tin.

'Thank you,' said Doris, looking pleased, but surprised.

Not half as surprised as Kenny. In the street, he hauled me up right away. 'Have you gone nuts?'

'No. It was payment.'

'Payment? What for?'

'Shush. Come down here.' I dragged him into a cobbled alley and round the back of the charity shop. It had a small paved yard with a tall wooden gate. I tried it. It was locked. I fell back against it.

Kenny looked at his watch. 'What are we doing?'

I waved him quiet. A door was opening at the back of the shop. Brief footsteps sounded, then the clatter I'd been hoping for: the lid of a skip being opened – and dropped.

Kenny worked it out. 'You're never gonna go for that stupid bear?'

'Leg me up,' I hissed, as the footsteps headed back the other way. He did, and I was over the wall in a flash. The skip was one of the plastic kind – more like a giant green treasure chest on wheels than the open-topped metal buckets builders use. I hid behind it till the shop lights dimmed. Then I opened the lid.

He was in a white bag with some jigsaws, near the top. It took me less than twenty seconds to pull him out, leap onto a dustbin and go.

'Joel,' Kenny panted, as we hit the park, running. 'This is totally, totally uncool. What're you gonna do with a teddy bear?'

He tried to punch it. I whisked the bear back. 'Draw him,' I said. 'For my coursework. For art.'

A faint light of understanding came into his eyes. He looked at my 'subject', shook his head and sighed. 'Why's it got a flag stuck under its arm?'

I lifted the arm. It was slack at the shoulder and almost came away. 'It's not a flag, it's a name badge, I think.' It was shiny and worn and I could barely read it. Just one word stood out: *Horace*. And a number: 012. 'He's called Horace,' I said and stroked the bear's nose.

Kenny looked like he might throw up. 'You've lost it, big time, Hadleigh.'

And he wasn't far wrong. If I'd known then the problems that bear was going to cause, I'd have left him in the skip and locked down the lid.

But I didn't. I smuggled him under my jacket. And then I took him home.

To trouble.

CHAPTER TWO

According to my dad, our house has 'the cleanest carpets in creation'. This is Dad's job: cleaning carpets. He runs his own business, out of the garage, sprucing up floors for offices and such. I never really think about it all that much, except when he's trying out another new solvent in the hall or the lounge or my bedroom, even. But that afternoon, I walked in on an argument that was going to bring all of us down to floor level – and Horace would soon be at the centre of it.

I didn't hear the whole thing, just a few snatches, as Kenny and I were coming up the garden.

'They just rang this afternoon and pulled the plug.' That was Dad, sounding pretty heated.

Mum hit back, 'Well, is it legal?'

'It's a free market, Emma. They can do what they like. That's what business is all about.'

'But you've had that contract with Bowmans for years. They must have given you *some* explanation?'

9

It stopped abruptly there. I heard Erin asking Mum if she'd seen her flute. She sounded puzzled – Erin, I mean. She'd be wondering, like me, why Mum and Dad were giving it out. Erin's the quiet one of the family, and quiet ones don't miss much.

Mum muttered something and Erin must have gone, 'cos Dad said 'flute' as if someone had hit him on the head with one.

'We're listing, not sinking,' Mum said tartly. 'We'll work it out, Trevor. We always do.'

At that point, me and Kenny walked into the kitchen.

'You pair are late tonight,' Mum breezed, dropping into 'mum' mode right away, as if she didn't have a worry in the world. Her gaze settled straight on the bear. 'Goodness, where *did* you get him?'

'He's in my class; he followed me home.' I shouldered Kenny onto a stool.

'Funnee,' said Mum, giving my hair a quick tousle.

I glanced up at Dad. He smiled at the joke, but I could see the concern in his close-set eyes. I knew he was wondering how much I'd heard.

'I'll be upstairs, making some calls,' he said, lobbing his car keys onto the table.

'Tea in half an hour,' Mum said, smiling. She was good at this, making trouble go away. I wanted to ask her why they'd been arguing, but she took Horace from me and talked about him. 'He needs mending, this bear – and he's *rather* grubby.' She started to tease up the flattened down fur.

'We got him from a charity shop,' said Kenny. 'Did Maddie go riding yet?'

As if by magic, my sister sauntered in. She was wearing a pair of tight blue jeans with a studded silver belt slung low across her hips. She's pretty, Maddie. Dark, like Mum. Same brown eyes and wavy hair. It suits the 'Goth' phase she's been going through lately. It suited Kenny, too. His eyes were nearly out on stalks as she sashayed by him, picking up a stick of celery to nibble. 'Mum, the shower's gone wrong,' she announced. 'Oh yuk, what's *that*?' She wrinkled her nose at Horace.

'Hi, Maddie,' said Kenny, before Mum could answer.

'Oh, hi,' she grunted, curling her lip.

'Aren't you going riding tonight?'

'Oh yeah, dressed like this!' With spiderweb tattoos on the backs of her hands and enough eyeliner to polish her shoes. 'Move your foot,' she said, poking it. 'I can't get to the fridge.'

Kenny moved his foot. 'Like your top,' he said. It was a black ribbed sweater with a high roll neck.

Maddie paused and took a long, deep breath. She hates it when Kenny tries to 'chat her up'. She's nearly fifteen now; Kenny's not. Even so he has this theory that one day she'll cave in and fall for his 'charms' (whatever they are). To be fair, he's quite good-looking, I suppose. Tall, fair-haired, big loopy grin. And lots of girls *do* like him (amazingly). But Maddie's got 'taste', or so she tells everyone – Kenny included, to his face.

'It's a sweater, OK?' she said with a scowl, and yanked the fridge open, rattling the contents. She pulled the straw off a small pack of juice, speared the box and started to drink.

'What are you going to call him, then?' asked Mum, bringing the subject back to the bear.

'His name's Horace,' I said. 'It's written underneath his arm.'

Mum tipped him up and squinted at the label. 'I think that's a manufacturer's tag. Horace and . . . *Sons* it looks like. Horace is a very good name for him, though.' She righted him again and he made a noise. 'Oh, he's got a growler.'

'A what?' I said.

Mum rocked him back and forth. On every third tip, the bear made a sort of baa-ing noise.

'Sounds like a sheep with laryngitis,' said Maddie.

Kenny stuck up his thumb. 'Yeah, good one.'

'Oh, purlease,' she moaned. 'Does he *have* to be here?'

'Hey, don't get peppy,' said Mum, dinking Maddie's nose with Horace's paw.

Maddie tightened in a flash and reeled away, crossing her arms, Egyptian mummy style. A host of bangles clattered to her elbows. 'Don't bring it near me; it might have fleas.'

Kenny immediately shook his head. 'Fleas only go for warm-blooded creatures. They wouldn't bite bears; they'd choke on the stuffing.'

'That's it,' said Maddie, pressing down on a pair of invisible dwarves. With a huff and a shudder she marched straight out.

Mum sighed and shook a despairing head. She often calls Maddie her 'slimline angel', but she'd gladly kick her off her cloud now and then. 'So, how much did you pay for Horace?'

'Fifty pence,' I said.

'Is that all?' Mum hollered, opening her eyes as big as pennies. The cry brought Erin into the kitchen.

'Hhh, a bear! Can I hold him, please?'

She took him anyway, hugging him as though he were a long-lost friend. 'Is he yours?' she asked Kenny, beaming at him. (This is the other complication between Kenny and my sisters: he likes Maddie, Erin likes him.)

'Don't be dumb,' he said.

'I'm not,' said Erin, in a chastening voice. 'I'm top of my year in five subjects, thank you.'

'That's put you in your place,' said Mum, tapping Kenny's head with a wooden spatula. She set a timer and left it ticking. 'I'm amazed you got Horace as cheaply as you did. Fifty pence is an absolute steal for a jointed bear like him.'

Kenny sat up, startled. 'We didn't nick it!'

I threw him a deadly, dangerous look. 'Fifty pence was all they wanted, *wasn't it?*'

'Erm, yeah,' he said quietly, biting his lip.

'He's sweet,' said Erin, waltzing him round. 'Can I have him?'

'No,' I said. 'I'm drawing him for art. How much would he really cost?' I asked Mum.

She picked up a tea towel and started drying pots. 'Ooh, I don't know. The bears you see in Lucan's in town fetch all sorts of fancy prices; forty or fifty pounds and more.'

'Fifty quid!' gasped Kenny. 'Wow. Let's go and sell him! Tomorrow!'

'No,' Erin tutted, holding Horace to her cheek. Her bobbed hair fell across his snout. 'He's lovely. He's ours.'

'He's mine,' I reminded her.

'You can't sell him,' she frowned.

'I agree,' said Mum. 'We haven't had a bear

in the family for years. He's beautiful. Do you want me to try and fix his arm?'

I shook my head. 'I want to draw him like he is.'

'What's for tea?' asked Kenny, getting bored.

'You, on a spit, if you're not careful,' said Mum. She took Horace from Erin and sat him on the worktop. 'All of you, off into the front room now. I've got things to do in here.'

'I'll go and see if Maddie's OK,' said Kenny, and he departed, Erin trailing after him.

At the door, I paused and looked back at Mum. 'Why were you arguing with Dad, just now?'

She glanced down and rubbed something clean on the sink. 'Your dad had a bad day at work, that's all. It's not the first time it's happened and it won't be the last.' She looked up and smiled. 'All right?'

I nodded and turned away. But as I climbed the stairs, I still felt anxious. One of the words I'd heard Mum use kept circling around in the top of my head: *listing*. In my bedroom, I looked it up. It meant to heel over, like a ship at sea, leaning or tilting in choppy waters. I didn't like the thought of my mum and dad 'tilting'. It made me wonder how far over they'd gone – and just how 'choppy' the waters were.

CHAPTER THREE

Over the weekend, all seemed normal. There were no more arguments. Life carried on. Maddie and Erin went out riding. Dad played golf. Mum laid her sewing stuff out in the lounge and worked on a costume of the Sheriff of Nottingham for a friend who was taking part in a pageant. And I stayed up in my room drawing Horace.

I drew him in pencils, in profile, first. A close-up, sitting in the bedroom window, staring out like a sailor home from sea, watching and waiting for the tide to roll in. His snout was very easy to draw, even the shiny balding patches where a few strands of hair had fallen out. It was pointed and long with good, clean angles, curving underneath into the base of his head. The ears were much harder and made me grizzle. It took me ages to get the shadowing right, to catch their size and cupped shape perfectly. His eyes were even worse. Mr Reynolds would have said they were melancholy eyes. Soulful. Distant.

Sombre. Pensive. These were the words he taught in Art. 'Feeling' words he called them. When we studied a subject – any subject – we had to try to interpret how 'it' was feeling, even if 'it' was a landscape or a vase. 'Let the emotions guide the hand.' That was Mr Reynolds' favourite quote. As I looked at Horace, staring away, the feeling that guided my hand was 'homesick'. Who could have dumped him in a charity shop? I wondered. A great old bear like him? OK, I'd never liked cuddly toys much. But Horace was different. Horace had style. Mum said he radiated 'old-fashioned charm'.

'Yes, I agree,' Mr Reynolds said, going through my roughs at school on Monday. 'Got something, hasn't he? A charisma. An allure.' He clicked his tongue as he said 'allure'. 'My partner, she likes bears, you know. Always studies their expressions before she buys. A bear's got to look right before she'll fork out. She takes ages about it; talks to them, too.'

'I don't talk to Horace, Mr Reynolds.'

He laughed and swung his cowboy boots off the desk. He'd been leaning backwards in an old wooden chair, shuffling my drawings like a thin pack of cards. He's not your normal teacher, Mr Reynolds. He has his hair swept back in a thin pony-tail, walks around in faded corduroy jeans and chews gum from start of school to stop. There's a rumour in our class that he might be a Country and Western singer.

'Where'd you get him, then?' he asked. 'Family heirloom, is he? Granny's old bear, dragged out of the attic?'

'Erm, yes,' I said, trying not to sound false. The fewer people who knew about the charity shop, the better.

Mr Reynolds nodded. 'Bet he's worth a bob or two.'

'Sir? He's dead old.'

'Exactly. That's the point. People are fond of collecting old things. He might be quite rare, for all you know. Bring him along to this Treasure thing on Friday, see what this Cholmondeley bloke has to say.'

He was talking about an event called 'Treasure Trove', which the school was hosting to raise money for African Water Relief. Some bloke called Christopher Cholmondeley (you pronounced it 'Chumley') had agreed to come in and value any 'antiques' we might have. Kenny had planned on taking in his *Star Wars* figures, until someone pointed out that you had to give a pound to the charity for each article valued (that would have cost him twenty-seven quid). But Horace was different. It would be worth a pound to find out something more about him. Bring him into school, though? That was dodgy. I'd be in blush city if my mates saw me toting a teddy bear around. I looked at Mr Reynolds and lifted my shoulders.

'Or the net,' he said. 'You could always try that. Do you know the manufacturer's name?'

I nodded.

'Bang it into a search engine, then. See what comes up.' He stood up and handed me my sketches back. 'Good work, Joel. Try another, face on.'

'OK,' I said, and hid away the drawings as the class poured in.

At dinner, I asked Kenny to come to the library and help me do what Mr Reynolds had suggested: look Horace up on the internet. But Kenny was in a strange kind of mood that day. All sort of starry-eyed and not quite there, as if someone had sucked his brain cells out and replaced them with washing-up suds or something. I left him chewing on the end of a ruler and went to the library alone.

Unusually, several machines were free, but I went to the two stuck away in the corner. (Looking up teddy bears was not très cool.) I logged on and clicked on a search tool. In the box that popped up I typed, *Horace and Sons*. Within seconds, a list of links had appeared. I didn't need to look any further than the first: *Manufacturers of quality, hand-crafted bears since ...*

I clicked and the screen filled up with info.

W. B. Horace and Sons began their family business in Withenshaw, near Manchester, in 1920, hand-crafting bears to be sold in fashionable outlets in and around their native Lancashire. But as the popularity of the new 'toys' grew, the business expanded into a world-wide enterprise and bears were soon being exported to all parts of the globe.

I clicked on an icon of a waving teddy and the screen began to fill with thumbnail images of various bears. As the last two or three were appearing, someone sat down at the machine beside mine. A girl. Her name was Roopindar Seehra. Her mates called her 'Roopi' or 'Roo' for short.

'Hi,' she whispered, spreading her lips to a very faint smile. She was in my year, so we knew one another. But that meant nothing; we hardly ever spoke. Out of politeness, I grunted back.

Strangely, this seemed to please her. A glint appeared in her huge round eyes and she sat up very straight and tall. Her black hair fell against her skinny brown arms, catching the fluorescent light from above. She glanced at my screen. I turned it away. She took the hint and didn't look again.

For the next ten minutes we sat there together, tapping and clicking, saying nothing. We didn't exchange another glance, but I could *feel* her presence all around me, as if she'd stepped outside her body and had draped herself over me like a coat.

Then, suddenly, her computer beeped and the next thing I knew she was bending to her ankles, zipping up her bag. She came up smiling, looping her hair. 'Bye,' she breathed, and gave a little wave.

'Bye,' I muttered, and watched her walk away. Despite the most enormous block-heeled shoes she managed to move with surprising elegance. She put a hand inside her hair and flicked it out. It shimmered from her neck right down to her waist. I was wondering if she'd ever had it cut when she glanced back briefly, over her shoulder. I switched my gaze very quickly to the screen.

I trawled through dozens and dozens of pics. There were lots of bears that resembled Horace, but none that looked exactly like him. I was just on the point of giving up when Kenny breezed in and sat on the chair Roopindar had left. He was nervous and grinning, tapping his toes. He looked at the bears but didn't comment.

'What's with you?' I asked.

'Say you won't laugh?'

'OK, I won't laugh. Ha. Ha. What have you done?'

'I'm going out,' he gulped. 'Y'know, with a girl.'

'Yeah, right.' I clicked on another pic.

He chewed his thumb and looked around the room. 'It's true. No kidding. She asked me at break.'

I let the mouse go. This was new. Kenny? Approached by a girl? 'Who?'

He swivelled his chair and his face began to flush. 'Laura.'

'Laura Brannigan?!'

'Zuzzzz,' he went, like a drunken bee. Every ear in the library tuned to our corner.

Now I couldn't help it. I had to hoot. 'Laura Brannigan wants to go out with you?'

He nodded and flapped me to keep my voice down.

'Don't be dumb. She's winding you up. She's posh, Laura Brannigan. She'll dump you the first time you scratch your bum. She won't go out with you.'

'She will. She is. Half past six tomorrow, on the park . . . but only as long as you come, too.'

'What?' My nose shortened into a sneer.

'Not just you. It's a foursome thing.'

'*What?!*'

'You, me, Laura and—'

'No.'

'Aw, Joel. Come on. You only have to walk with her.'

'No.' I logged off and grabbed my bag. 'Who?' I was curious.

'Laura's mate.'

'Yeah, obviously. Who's Laura's mate?'

His hands whirled like the blades of a mixer. 'Whassaname. Y'know. Dead long hair.'

'Roopindar?' My insides started to coil.

Kenny grinned and stuck up his thumbs. 'Kangaroo girl, yeah. She won't give you any grief. All you've gotta do is walk with her . . .'

CHAPTER FOUR

Somehow, I let him talk me into it. But I insisted on three unbreakable conditions: one, he supported me when I brought Horace into school on Friday (I'd decided by then that I would); two, he did not tell *anyone*, especially my parents, that I was going on a 'date' (I wasn't, I was just his chaperone, *remember*?); and three, we played it totally cool.

He agreed to every condition on the spot – and blew the last of them before we'd even started.

He turned up at my house at six the next night and perched on the orange settee in the front room. Maddie was the first to notice him.

She walked in, heading for the music system, stopped in the centre of the floor and turned. Her mouth fell open and she gawped at Kenny. 'You smell,' she said.

Most lads would have chucked abuse at her for that, but Kenny, being Kenny, in the presence of my sister, grinned and said, 'It's *Voodoo Warrior*; my dad's aftershave.'

Daggers came winging out of my eyes.

'I only dabbed a bit on, honest,' he said.

Maddie's mouth cocked into a sneer. 'You? Shave?'

'He started last week,' I told her quickly, before she could work out the real reason Kenny was daubing his mug with pong. 'He's doing it just to show off, *aren't you*?'

'Do you like it?' he asked her.

She pulled her grossest girly face. 'Excuse me? You *reek*.'

'I think that's Mum's deodorant,' he said, undoing his shirt and having a sniff.

Maddie shuddered and looked as if she might just heave.

'I'm going upstairs to get a jumper,' I said, and left them to it: Kenny sniffing at his chest and armpits; Maddie tucked up in a chair in the corner, hidden tight behind one of her mags.

In my bedroom, Erin was waiting. This wasn't unexpected. We're close, me and Erin. We talk about stuff. We don't keep secrets. Although I don't bother with her room much, she's free to spend time in mine if she wants to. She was sitting on the bed, leaning back against the wall, cuddling Horace and smoothing his ears. 'Are you going out?'

'To the park, that's all.'

She raised her eyes coyly. 'To see a girl?'

'E-*rin*. Don't be dumb.'

'Kenny's all dressed up.' She put her chin on Horace's head and rocked him quietly from side to side.

I knew I would have to tell her then. She adored Kenny. She'd be hurting a bit. 'He's seeing a girl from our year. Nothing special.'

'What's her name?'

'Laura Brannigan. Erin, you don't know her.'

She sat still a moment, peering into space, checking her extensive 'people' database. She might only be eleven, but her brain has the power of a super-computer. 'That blond-haired girl with the ski-run nose who carries her books in a *Mister Man* bag?'

Honestly, we ought to have christened her 'Sherlock'. 'Yes,' I said.

'That's all right then.' She smiled and gave Horace an extra squeeze.

I pulled a black sweater out of a drawer. 'How do you mean?'

'No, not that one,' she flapped. 'The blue one; it matches your eyes much better.'

'Uh?'

'The *blue* one.' She poked my arm.

Frowning, I turned to the drawer and swapped.

'What's *your* girl called?'

'Me? I haven't got one.'

'Joel . . .' She sighed and her gaze went rigid. I hate it when she does this to me. Her eyeballs turn to big blue marbles and you know, you just *know* she's figured you're lying. Moving a strand of hair from her mouth, she explained, perfectly, how it would be: 'If you and Kenny are going together, Laura must be bringing her mate along. That's the way it works.'

'How would *you* know?'

'Girls do. We're smart. What's her name?'

I pulled on the dark blue sweater. 'Roopindar.'

'She's Asian?'

'Yes.'

'Is she pretty?'

'No, she's got goofy teeth, glasses and she walks with a limp.'

'Fibber. Asian girls are *always* pretty.' She grinned wickedly and rocked Horace some more, shaking some stuffing from the ever-growing tear between his limp arm and his chest.

This time, I lobbed a question at her. 'What did you mean when you said it was all right for Kenny to be meeting Laura Brannigan?'

Her gaze fell sideways.

'Tell me – or I'll tickle.'

'No.' She clutched Horace and his growler baa-ed.

'Tell me or it's monsters of the coral reef . . .'
I wriggled my fingers, making her squirm.

'Joel, stop it. Don't be horrible.'

'Spill, then.'

'No.'

Too bad. I lunged.

She squealed then and cried out all in one breath: 'No don't she's just not right for him that's all!'

I paused, fingertips on her waist. 'She must like him or she wouldn't have asked him to meet her.'

She shied away, glowering, tidying her hair. 'Maybe. Or they could be planning something.'

'Such as? And what do you mean by "they"?'

'Don't know,' she said and quickly changed the subject. 'Did you get Mum a thimble, yet?'

That was a killer. I stopped thinking of the park and thought of the hunt. 'No,' I confessed.

Erin wriggled her way to the front of the bed. 'You can share in mine if you want to, you know.'

And she meant it. She was kind like that. I was about to say I hadn't finished looking yet when she switched again, to something much thornier. 'Dad's accountant is coming round tonight.'

I looked at her carefully. She had a lovely, fair-skinned, innocent face that you knew would be truly beautiful one day. Right now, though, worry lines were spoiling her brow. She'd picked up on the 'listing' ship. So it hadn't gone away. I wondered what she knew.

'Dad's got a cashflow problem,' she said.

She was quoting from overheard speech, that was obvious. Bright as she was, she wouldn't have understood the ins and outs of business talk. I didn't understand it much myself, but 'cashflow' didn't take a lot of working out: Dad was short of money.

'How do you know?'

'I heard him telling Mum in the bedroom. When he went out, she looked at her thimbles.'

'Why?'

'I don't know.'

'She looked at her *thimbles*?'

Erin nodded slowly and chewed her hair. 'I think she's going to sell them.'

CHAPTER FIVE

'You gonna buy me an ice-cream, then?' Laura Brannigan floated through the air on a swing, one toe poking suggestively at Kenny as she made each gentle upward rise.

Kenny looked across the park at the Percy's van, waiting for business out on the road. He shook his head. 'You can't eat *Percy's* ice-cream.'

'Why not?' Laura looked a bit cheesed off.

Kenny shrugged as if everyone knew why not. 'Old man Percy stirs it with his foot.'

'*What?*' Laura brought her swing to a clanking halt and stared in disgust at the ice-cream van. The young bloke in the driver's seat, uncannily aware that he was being watched, glanced sideways at her and flicked a cigarette butt onto the pavement.

'Me and Joel were the ones who sussed it,' said Kenny. 'We found some toenail in a cornet once.'

On the stone wall beside me, Roopindar winced.

'It was old and grey. From his biggie, we reckoned.'

'That's disgusting. Please tell me he's lying,' said Roo.

I shook my head. Bizarrely, it was true. My cornet, too. Totally revolting.

'He stirs his sweat in as well,' said Kenny. 'That's what makes it creamy, like sick.'

'Ugh,' went Laura, flapping her fists.

'And his chocolate flakes are made from—'

'Shut up! I'll have a lolly instead – and not a *Percy's* one, OK?'

Kenny frowned and felt his pockets. I could see this was something of a learning curve for him: if you went out with girls, it cost you money.

'I'll choose,' said Laura, leaping off the swing. She looped Kenny's arm and tugged him away.

I sighed and slid off the wall to follow. This had been the pattern of the 'date' so far: wherever Kenny and Laura went, me and Roopindar had to tag along behind. Only this time Roopindar didn't move. And when Laura saw me coming she was quick to wag a finger. I sat back on the wall again, bored.

After a while, Roopindar spoke: 'Like your sweater.'

I let my gaze drop to my chest.

'Matches your eyes,' she said.

Eyes? Sweater? Hadn't Erin just said the same thing at home? I shuffled uncomfortably and stared at the ground.

Roopindar gathered up a handful of hair and started to examine the ends for splits. 'You don't say much, do you?'

I shrugged and bounced my heels off the wall. I was only here to make up the numbers. So was she. What was there to say?

'You look as if something's bothering you.'

Yeah, well. She wasn't wrong there. I'd been thinking about what Erin had said from the moment we'd all set foot on the park. Mum couldn't sell her *thimbles*. Never. No way.

'I'm not prying, y'know. Just talking, that's all. Passes the time while we wait for them, doesn't it?'

I didn't know what to say.

She let her hair drop and strummed it like a harp. 'Is it something to do with school?'

'Uh, what?'

'What's bugging you? Is it school?'

'No. It's . . . my mum.'

'What's wrong with her? She sick?'

'No.' This was dumb. Why was I discussing Mum with this . . . girl?

I looked up to see how Kenny was doing. He had his back to me still, buying the lollies. Laura, one foot pressed against the van, was focusing hard on me and Roopindar. I noticed she'd done this several times, passing girly messages with her eyes. There was something I couldn't quite pin down here, especially about the way they were dressed. Roopindar was wearing a black denim jacket with matching jeans and a turquoise top that showed her bare waist whenever she stretched. Laura had arrived in an anorak and joggers. Why was the posh girl looking like a scarecrow while her tag-along mate was dressing so cool?

'She giving you grief or something?'

'Who?' I said.

'Your mum!' Roopindar cried, splaying her hands and muttering in Punjabi under her breath. 'Honestly, my rabbit's more talkative than you.'

'I don't think so,' I said.

'Wow,' she came back, dropping her jaw. 'Four words. A whole sentence. Wow.'

'OK, don't get sarky. I'm trying to find a special present for her birthday. It's on Friday; I haven't got her anything yet.'

Progress. A sympathetic light shone out of her eyes. Wedging her hands between her thighs she asked, 'Is that why you were looking at bears in the library?'

Drat. She'd noticed. Now I felt the blood

rushing into my cheeks. 'That was a project for art, OK?'

'OK,' she repeated in mock surrender. She angled her foot, letting her heel slip out of her shoe. 'What kind of things does she like, your mum?'

'Thimbles.' I told her about the hunt.

'That's sweet,' she came back. 'Every year? You never miss?'

'No – except this year. Don't s'pose you know where I can find one – a good one?'

She thought about it, swaying like a blade of grass. 'I could ask my uncle; he works the markets.'

'Really?'

'You want it for Friday, yeah?'

Three short days. I nodded. 'Yeah.'

She jumped off the wall and swiped her bum. 'OK, I'll try. No promises, though. Come on, the others are here.'

Kenny and Laura swaggered up, laughing – feeding each other their lollies. Gross.

'Where's mine?' I asked.

Kenny wiped his orange-stained mouth on his sleeve. 'You never asked for one. He's gone now, anyway.'

'Me, too,' said Roopindar. 'I've gotta go. Soz.'

'Oh, Roo?' Laura frowned at her, hard.

'Homework,' she said. 'Mum and Dad don't like me doing it late.'

Kenny squinted at the pavilion clock. 'It's only ten past seven.'

'I do extra classes. Joel, would you walk me back to my house?'

Laura's mouth fell open like a bucket.

'It's not far. See you tomorrow, Laura.'

'Too right,' she said, breaking into a snort.

I glared at Kenny. He shrugged and gave me a sheepish grin.

Cheers, Kenny. Some mate *you* are. Landed. With a girl.

Just walking.

Right.

She lived on one of the posh estates, just over the hill from Ottley, our school. On the way, we talked about football, of all things. She didn't seem to understand much about the game (at one point she asked me, 'Who holds the corner flag?'). I wondered why she'd bothered to start on football if she was going to be as dumb as that. So I did most of the talking for her – till we reached her house, anyway. Then her dad took over. He was outside, pruning a privet bush. He was a great big bear of a bloke in a light grey shirt and a dark blue turban. He had a fantastic beard, thick and wiry like a squirrel's nest. The ends of his moustache were almost as big as the curtain tie-backs in our lounge.

'Roopindar, what do you think?' he said, in a cheery, booming voice. 'Your mother wants to see more curves in the garden. This is my attempt at a jolly peacock.'

Roopindar smiled and took her dad's arm. 'This is Joel, Papa-ji. He's an artist. Ask him.'

Mr Seehra grinned with delight. He had massive teeth and huge pink gums. 'Joel, what do you say? Should I take a little more off the silly bird's head?'

I looked at the bush. At the moment, the 'peacock' resembled a pear. I told him, honestly. He laughed out loud.

'Then we will have a fruit garden instead!'

I waved at Roopindar and started to go.

'Thanks for walking me home,' she said. She smiled shyly and nibbled her lip.

'I should be the one saying that,' said her dad. He looked me up and down and nodded his approval. 'So, this is the young man we hear so much about?'

'DAD!' Roopindar's hands shot straight to her face. She turned and scurried away into the house.

'Oh dear,' Mr Seehra said.

Oh dear indeed. The tips of my ears were beginning to flare, and with the heat came a great big blush of understanding. The clothes, the lollies, all the silly talk home. It wasn't Kenny and Laura who'd been 'dating' on the park; that was just a scam, like Erin had suggested. It had all been a set-up, organized by Laura – to push me and Roopindar Seehra together.

CHAPTER SIX

Friday came. Mum's forty-second birthday. Every year she tells us not to make a fuss and to leave present-giving till after school, and every year it's exactly the same: we pile her presents on the kitchen table and make her open every one at breakfast. Dad, as always, had bought her a massive bunch of flowers, and this year some perfume and a new pair of boots. For their presents, the girls had clubbed together and bought Mum a CD and some blobby little earrings that Erin said were 'haematite' and Maddie insisted had come from a meteor crash in Russia and were radioactive and would probably make Mum glow in the dark (Maddie is dippy like that sometimes). I gave Mum a poetry book that I'd seen her reading in a shop in town and a bagful of her favourite black wine gums (I'd been buying ordinary wine gums for weeks and putting all the black ones aside, because black are the only colour she likes). And everyone, of course, had bought her a thimble.

Except me – I'd made one from a piece of

card. I'd drawn a cutesy picture of Horace on it and written in really tiny letters *We O. U. a proper one, soon*. It made Mum cry. She hugged me so tight that I thought I could hear my neck bones cracking. She said if I never bought another one again, this little thimble (she waggled it on her finger) would be priceless and take prime position in her set. And I don't know why I said it, I just couldn't help myself; I asked, 'Mum, how much are your thimbles worth?' And a new tear welled up over the first. Erin stiffened and looked towards Dad.

He bent down, kissed Mum's head and answered, 'More than money could buy, Joel.' Mum reached for his hand and he kissed hers romantically, making Maddie flutter her lashes. 'Going to see a man about a dog,' he whispered. He put a waft of Mum's hair behind her ear and let his hand drape smoothly over her neck. He kissed Maddie, kissed Erin, knuckled my arm and walked down the hall without another word.

Upstairs, afterwards, Erin nearly killed me. 'Why did you go and ask Mum *that*?' She stormed in while I was dressing for school.

I turned away, embarrassed. 'It just came out.'

'You know *why* she was crying, don't you? She wants to sell her thimbles to help Dad's business, but *he* won't let her, because they're so precious. How could you *say* that? On her birthday, too!'

'I couldn't help it, OK? It just came out!' I flapped at my tie and the knot fell apart.

Erin tutted and started to tie it for me. 'I think Dad's going to the bank today.'

I groaned and asked her how she knew that.

'Didn't you hear? He's going to see a man about a dog. That doesn't mean he's buying us a puppy, Joel. It means he's meeting someone important, like a solicitor or a bank manager or an insurance salesman; he's probably going to talk about the cashflow problem.'

'Erin, will you shut up about that. We're OK, aren't we? Nothing's changed.' It had been a week now since I'd overheard the argument. Apart from Dad being bogged down in paper-work, everything seemed to be cosy enough.

Not for Erin. 'Something's wrong,' she insisted, jamming the tied knot into my throat. 'Mum made a shopping list last night.'

'So?'

'She *never* makes a list. It means she's being careful about what she buys. And I saw her staring through the kitchen window. She only does that when she's really worried.'

'I've got to go,' I sighed, and reached for Horace. He was in a carrier bag on my bed.

'Where are you taking him?'

'School.'

'What for?'

'To show someone.'

'Who? Roopindar?'

'No,' I snapped, almost biting off her nose. I hadn't seen Roopindar, apart from glimpses, since the night she'd run in flushed from her dad's comment.

Erin ran a finger down Horace's ear. 'Why won't you tell me what happened on the park?'

I moved her aside to get to my books. 'We sat on the swings, talked a bit, went home.'

'She likes you, doesn't she?' she stated boldly, in that strange unnerving way she has of getting right to the core of the truth.

'Erin?!' This time, the voice wasn't mine. Mum was calling up from the bottom of the stairs. 'Come on, your porridge is going cold!'

Erin turned on her heels and marched towards the door. 'I'll find out. I always do.'

And that scared me, for two good reasons. One, she always *did* find out; and two, I had the uneasy feeling she was probably right about Roopindar.

CHAPTER SEVEN

The appeal for African Water Relief had raised a huge buzz of support in school. After the final bell that Friday, the hall was overflowing with kids. Stalls had been set out all around the walls, spilling out into the yard as well. Everything from face-painting to balloon-racing to penalty-taking to cake-baking – not forgetting the star attraction, Christopher Cholmondeley and his 'Treasure Trove'.

Me and Kenny were in the car park when he arrived. He drove up in a bright red, open-topped sports car that almost filled two parking bays. He reminded me a bit of an old-fashioned cricketer, tall and pale-faced, with slicked-back hair and glasses that had no frames around the lenses. His cream flannel trousers billowed when he walked. A hankie arrowed out of his blazer pocket. He asked us, brusquely, to show him to the hall. We led the way, where he was greeted by our Head, Mr Grace, and Mrs Tulip who took us for history and German.

'Delighted. Perfectly delighted,' said Cholmondeley, clasping rather than shaking hands. 'Now, then, where would you like me, eh?'

Mrs Tulip fluttered like a sparrow and pointed to the stage where a table, covered in soft green baize, had been set aside in front of the piano.

'Excellent,' Christopher Cholmondeley said. He took a watch from his pocket and focused back and forth like he was playing the trombone. 'I have a pressing appointment at five. Send the first one up.' And he whisked across the hall with such devastating speed that Mrs Tulip was almost blown over by the blast. Children parted from his path like waves spraying out from the bow of a ship. I decided at once that I hated him.

But I'd put my name on the list to see him. I'd paid my pound and I didn't want to waste it. It was half an hour, though, before my slot came up.

'Duncan Fry!' Mr Grace announced. 'I hope you've brought your auntie's teapot! You're next, after Avril, to see Mr Cholmondeley.' A ripple of laughter ran around the hall as Duncan took his place in the Treasure Trove queue. Mr Grace ticked him off the list. 'After Duncan, Joel Hadleigh, please – with "Horace", whoever "Horace" is.'

'I've seen it; it's a teddy bear!' someone

shouted, and the place erupted with laughter again. Worse than that, kids began to flock to me from all directions.

'Fifty pence a look!' Kenny said, to warn them off. Nice try, but it didn't work. Within seconds me and Horace were completely surrounded. Someone tore the carrier bag. Then it started:

Aah, look. Do you sleep with it, Joel?

Where's your pram, Joel?

Did you go down to the woods today, Joel?

I was just about to sock the next joker in the mouth when a voice said, 'He's lovely. Is he really yours?' A small brown hand stroked Horace's muzzle. Roopindar.

She was wearing her hair tied back off her face, so her eyes, when she opened them, were almost as wide as oyster shells. 'I just came to tell you there's something on the Bring and Buy your mum might like. Bye.' And that was it. She flexed her fingers and walked away.

Kenny gave a thoughtful sniff. 'I think she fancies you, you know.'

'Shut up,' I hissed. I was red enough already. 'Go and look for that thimble. Quick.'

'What thimble?'

'The one she's just been talking about. At the park, I told her about Mum's collection; she must have seen one on the stall. Go and bag it.'

'No, I want to see what happens with Horace.'

He nodded at the table. Duncan was about to take his place.

'He'll be ages, Kenny. I *need* that thimble.'

With a sigh of submission, he held out his hand. 'Givus some money, then.'

I felt my pockets. 'Can't, I'm skint. Ask whoever's on the stall to put the thimble aside.'

Kenny glanced over. 'Aw, no. It's Laura. She split with me this morning.'

Before I could comment, he'd piped up again. 'It's OK, though. It was cool. We're gonna stay mates. And I only went out with her to gain experience—'

'What?'

'– so I'd know what to do with Maddie—'

'What?!'

'– you didn't *tell* Maddie, did you? About me and Laura? I don't want her to think I was two-timing her.'

'Kenny!' My snap carried right across the hall, making a clown spill his juggling balls. 'You can't two-time someone you're not even one-timing.'

He twisted his nose in the way that he does when he's picking it or thinking hard (allegedly). 'I know, but you have to have aspirations. It was on my mum's *Thought for the Day* calendar this morning. Have aspirations. It means to keep wishing for what you want.'

'Put a brain at the top of the list, then, you moron. Maddie will *never* go out with you.'

'And faith,' he said. 'That's tomorrow's thought.'

'Kenny, if you don't go and save that thimble, you might not live to *see* tomorrow!'

I pointed to the stall. Finally, he went.

At the same moment, a deep groan from Christopher Cholmondeley drew my attention back to the table. Duncan and his teapot were being waved away. 'It's not worth the glue it's held together with, I'm afraid. And I wouldn't make any tea in it, either, unless you want to see it in pieces. Next!'

Duncan retreated, looking stupid. Nervously, I climbed the steps to the stage. Mr Cholmondeley gave a tired glance sideways. He saw Horace through the rips of the carrier bag and sighed. 'Teddy bear,' he said, as if swilling a foul taste round his mouth. He folded his arms and leaned back in his chair, pressing his thick lips tightly together.

I drew Horace out. 'Yes, he's . . . my gran's.'

'They always are, dear boy. They always are. Well, turn it around. Let's see what we've . . .' Suddenly, his words petered out to a dot and a hungry kind of light went on in his eyes. Lifting his spectacles off his chest (they were tied to a loop of cord around his neck), he pulled Horace forward and examined him closely, eyes roving over the underarm label. 'Granny's bear, you say?'

I murmured a yes.

He lowered his specs to his chest again. 'How old is Granny, exactly?'

I shrugged. How should I know? Ancient. 'Why?'

Christopher Cholmondeley didn't answer. He fiddled in his pocket for a magnifying glass and used that to study Horace's label. 'Did she buy him or was he handed down?'

'Don't know,' I said. I wished I'd never mentioned Gran at all. Every lie I had to invent just made me feel more and more on edge. It didn't help that Mr Grace had just sauntered up.

'Only two to go, Christopher. Not been too bad a trial, I hope?'

Cholmondeley sat back, drumming his fingers. 'On the contrary, it's proving quite fascinating, Edmund. Quite, quite fascinating.'

'Lovely bear, Joel,' Mr Grace said, smiling. 'How much did you—?'

'Gentlemen, I'm afraid you must excuse me.' Christopher Cholmondeley flapped a hand, cutting Mr Grace off dead. 'I've just remembered I have a dreadfully urgent phone call to make.' He reached into his blazer and pulled out a mobile. 'I'll pop outside. I do apologize for this.' He touched my arm and patted Horace's head. 'Don't run away, either of you.' And coughing deep into the folds of his handkerchief, he powered off towards the nearest exit.

Bewildered, I sat there wondering what to do. I was still looking around when Kenny bowled up with Mr Reynolds. 'Did you get it?' I asked.

Kenny opened his hand. In the centre of his palm was a white ceramic thimble painted with a neat oriental pattern. Yes! I'd done it. I'd kept my birthday contract with Mum.

'Cost twenty pence. I haggled,' he said.

Laughing, Mr Reynolds put the thimble on his finger. 'Taking up sewing now, boys?'

'No,' we both said in perfect unison. I explained about Mum's birthday and the search we'd had.

'You were lucky, finding one today, then,' he said. He put it on the green baize, next to Horace.

I ran my thumb around the smooth white rim. Yes, it was lucky. Incredibly lucky. I supposed I ought to thank Roopindar for spotting it. I could see her browsing the second-hand book-stall. My stomach fluttered and I didn't know why.

'Where's our antiques expert then?' Mr

Reynolds had picked up the magnifying glass and was training it on the empty chair.

'Gone outside to make a phone call, sir.'

'What did he say about Horace?' asked Kenny.

I lifted my shoulders. 'Nothing yet. He just looked at his label and asked a few questions. Then he said he needed to ring someone.'

Mr Reynolds glanced through the long hall windows. 'About the bear?'

'Don't think so,' I said. In the yard, Christopher Cholmondeley was grinding a cigarette under his heel and talking rapidly into his phone.

Mr Reynolds recorded a thoughtful hum. 'He's coming back,' he said, and stepped away from the table.

Seconds later, Cholmondeley was pounding up the stage steps. 'Now, then. Where the devil were we?' he said, clapping his hairy hands together. 'Ah yes, this fascinating bear.'

Right on cue, Mr Grace drifted forward. 'CC, if you're pushed for time we could cancel the last two—'

'No, no. I'd like to say something about this item.' 'CC' turned his chair around and sat astride it with his elbows resting on the back. He clamped me dead in the eye. 'How much do you think this bear is worth?'

'Fifty quid at least,' Kenny said right away.

'Be quiet,' said Mr Grace. 'He's asking Joel.'

Mr Cholmondeley leaned forward. 'Shall I tell you, Joe? Would you like to know?'

I hated people calling me Joe, but I nodded anyway. I hadn't paid my pound just to watch him smoke a fag.

He smiled and removed his glasses, hooking one arm of them over his lip. 'In good condition, at auction, he would fetch somewhere in the region of two hundred and fifty pounds . . .'

'Wow!' went Kenny.

'Goodness me,' said Mr Grace.

I looked at Mr Reynolds. His eyebrows lifted but he didn't say a word.

'There, what do you think about that?'

Frightened, that's what I thought about that. Any minute now I expected the cops to come rushing in and arrest me for thieving from a charity shop. Was it thieving? Lifting from a skip? I had *tried* to pay for Horace, but not as much as . . .

'Two hundred and fifty,' Mr Cholmondeley bragged, staring like a cobra into my eyes. He drew the figure invisibly with his finger. 'Two hundred and fifty *pounds*.'

'Impressive,' said a voice. 'Let's hope his drawings are worth as much one day.' Mr Reynolds bustled forward and thrust a piece of paper into my hand. 'Here's that sketch you left with me, Joel. Study my suggestions carefully, won't you?'

'Sketch?' I muttered. I had no idea what he was talking about.

'Mr Reynolds, this is not the time for class,' said Mr Grace.

'Quite right. My apologies, Head. When you've had a quick look, fold that up and put it away, Joel. Come and see me about it on Monday, though, will you?'

'Yes, sir,' I muttered, peeking at the paper. I folded it slowly and stuffed it in my pocket.

Mr Reynolds winked at me once, then faded into the crowd.

Mr Cholmondeley tapped my arm. 'Tell me something, Joe—'

'His name's Joel,' said Kenny.

Cholmondeley pulled a shirt cuff clear of his blazer and slanted Kenny a threatening look. 'How attached is Grandma to the bear, *Joel*?'

'Why?' I asked in a timid voice.

He sat back, slowly lacing his fingers. 'I'll be perfectly frank: I'd like to buy him off you.'

'Good Lord,' said Mr Grace, snapping the tip of his pencil in shock.

Mr Cholmondeley wagged a hesitant finger. 'Not for two-fifty, I hasten to add. I'm afraid he's well past his prime and worth little more than . . . sixty—'

'Is that all?' sneered Kenny.

'-- maybe seventy-five,' Mr Cholmondeley growled.

Mr Grace whistled. 'Still a healthy amount.'

'Quite,' said Cholmondeley, with a denture-packed smile. 'Though seventy is nearer the mark, I think.'

I looked at him blankly.

His slick stare crept into the depths of my skull. 'Seventy pounds is a fair price, Joel. But I think I'm sensing some hesitancy in you. Not really surprising, I suppose. Grandma's bear? The dust of her life in his creaking joints? Bound to be a certain sentimental fondness.' A finger sprang upright out of his fist. He lowered his voice to a notch above a whisper. 'However, I'm going to be candid with you. This bear is in a somewhat shabby state. Maybe Granny hasn't given him all the love he deserves? Not as devoted as she once was, perhaps?' He paused and his voice rose again. 'He needs a good home, Joel. And I happen to know a delightful young lady who would offer him that. I have a friend whose daughter adores old teddies.' He leaned so close I could smell his mouthwash. 'You may think this rather odd, but she's blind—'

'How's she going to see it then?' Kenny butted in.

Mr Cholmondeley slapped a palm down on

the table. 'With her hands, you idiot. She can picture him by feeling his curves and contours. I'm sure an artist like Joel can appreciate that.'

He smiled at me, hoping for some kind of answer. When I didn't give one, he pursed his lips and pulled a swollen wallet from the depths of his jacket. 'Here's seventy pounds. Seventy-five. I'll be generous.' He counted it out on the table in front of me. 'Isn't that a fair exchange? All these notes for that tatty old thing and the joy of a poor, unfortunate girl?'

I looked at the money and shook my head.

Kenny made a kind of snorting sound and gripped the back of my chair for support.

With eyes as cold and deadly as a hawk's, Christopher Cholmondeley studied me hard. 'Yes, I understand. This is a little mercenary on my part, isn't it?'

Was it? I hadn't got a clue what he meant.

'I'm forgetting the whole point of today's appeal: we're here to aid those less privileged, aren't we?'

I nodded. It seemed the right thing to do.

The wallet flexed open again. 'So what if I said that I will not only give you that money for the bear' – he pushed the nest of notes across the baize towards me – 'but I'll match it pound for pound with a donation to the school charity?'

'My word!' Mr Grace exclaimed. 'That's

remarkably munificent, CC. Think of all the clean water that could provide in Africa, Joel? What do you say?'

'He's not for sale.' I picked Horace up and pressed him to my hip.

A dark spear pierced Mr Cholmondeley's eyes. 'There's no need to be hasty,' he breathed.

'I'm going now. Thanks.'

'Wait,' he cried. 'What about a hundred?' A few more notes fell onto the table.

'He's not for sale – to anyone,' I said. I stood up and clattered down the steps. Away.

Kenny caught up with me out in the yard. 'Joel, slow down. Gracie's going bonkers. Why didn't you take the dosh?! We could have been *rich*.'

I pulled Mr Reynolds' sheet of paper from my pocket. 'Look at that.'

'Your drawing?'

'It's not a drawing. *Look*.'

When he opened it, his face became a maze of confusion. 'What does it mean?'

'What it says, you dunce.'

Mr Reynolds had written four words on the paper.

DON'T SELL THE BEAR.

CHAPTER EIGHT

That night, my parents made their grand announcement. Erin had got it completely right. Dad *had* been to the bank, and there *was* a problem. And now we were going to be told about it.

As soon as Maddie came home from drama class, they gathered all three of us into the lounge.

'Sit down,' said Dad. He was going to do the talking.

'What's the matter?' asked Maddie. 'What did we do?'

'Nothing. You're not in trouble,' said Mum. 'Just listen to your dad. This is very important.'

All three of us settled onto the sofa. Me in the middle. My sisters to the sides. Erin fidgeted away from something in my pocket. The thimble. I hadn't had a chance to present it to Mum yet.

Dad took a deep breath and turned to face us. 'I wouldn't normally tell you something like this, but it affects us all and it's only right that you should know. My business has hit a few problems. A company whose offices I've cleaned for many years has decided not to employ me any more—'

'Why?' asked Maddie, cutting in with her usual petulant frown.

'I don't know,' Dad replied calmly. He held her gaze for a second or two, then looked at me, and then at Erin. 'To make matters worse, a short while ago I borrowed . . . an amount of money from the bank. I raised this loan on the assumption that I'd have enough work to pay it off comfortably. Now the work isn't there any more.'

'You mean we're poor?' Maddie looped her hair and looked searchingly at Mum.

'We have to make a few changes,' said Mum. I could see a film of moisture building up in her eyes. It would have been enough to silence me or Erin, but Maddie still had to probe.

'Changes?' She said it with a harshness that made Mum look away. Maddie turned her brooding glare on Dad.

'We're not poor,' he said, 'but we will be if we don't adapt to this challenge.'

'Adapt?' Maddie seemed to know all the key words to pick. She threw it back at Dad with open-mouthed lippiness.

'We need to make savings – a lot of them,' he said, somehow keeping his temper in check.

'Our resources are going to be stretched to the limit. I'm afraid your allowances will have to stop.'

Maddie's jaw dropped open in smooth slow-motion. 'No money?' she breathed.

'Less money,' said Dad, 'controlled by me and your mum.'

Maddie blinked in shock. But there was worse to come.

'And we can't afford to send you riding for a while.'

'What?'

'Or to flute classes, Erin. Or dance or drama,' he said to Maddie. 'Or trips to see the City,' he said to me.

'No, this is horrible!' Maddie protested, balling her fists up tightly in her lap. 'You're my dad. You're *supposed* to give us things.'

'I'm supposed to look after you the best way I can.'

'Well, get another job, then!'

'Maddie?' I growled.

Dad raised a hand, telling me to calm it. 'I'm already seeking a new batch of clients. But it won't be easy to re-establish a contract as lucrative as the one I've just lost. In the meantime, while things remain unsettled, your mum is going to start looking for a job.'

Erin and I both turned to her, gaping. Mum

had *never* gone out to work. She had enough on her plate just coping with us, and Dad had always been proud of the fact that he was the one who supported us all.

'The routine is going to change,' he said.

Erin, not listening, was focusing her wide blue eyes on Mum. 'Can't you just make more costumes?' she asked.

Coming from Erin, this was a deeply naïve sort of question. We all knew Mum made a little bit of 'pocket money' from her sewing, but there was never enough there for a regular wage.

She reached out and covered Erin's hand. 'No.'

'You're serious, aren't you?' Maddie panted lightly. She was staring blindly at the carpet now. 'You really, really mean it. You're really going to stop our allowances, aren't you?'

'Yes,' said Dad.

Then came the breaking point. Erin, knotting her fingers, said, 'Please don't sell your thimbles, Mummy.'

Mum's head went down and she covered her eyes. Erin was off the settee in a flash. Maddie, too. But she wasn't running to hug anyone. Crying, 'I hate you!' over and over, she blasted through the door and out into the hall.

'Maddie?' Dad strode to the doorway after her.

'Leave me alone! I hate you!' she yelled. We heard her pounding up the stairs. Somewhere near the top, she stopped to shout: 'I'm not missing drama class, even if you—'

And then came the shriek and the awful rumble: teenage bones on carpeted wood; the crash of a vase as her body reached the bottom. She would tell us later that during her run, her shoe had flown off like Cinderella's slipper and her stockinged heel had slipped on the fan of the stairs. But right then, all we knew was the fall.

'MADDIE!' Mum and Dad screamed together.

When I got into the hall she lay crumpled on the floor, one leg tucked half under the other. Four or five drops of bright red blood had spotted the skirting at the bottom of the stairs. One arm was stretched out, palm up, still. A tear-stained, peach-coloured, scrunched-up tissue lay like a broken flower beside it. I couldn't see her face, it was hidden by Dad's. He was down on his knees and bending over her – giving her the kiss of life.

CHAPTER NINE

In the art room on Monday, I kept my appointment with Mr Reynolds and brought him up to date with what had happened at the Treasure Trove on Friday.

'*Aiding those less privileged,*' he scoffed, echoing Christopher Cholmondeley's words. 'Lining his greedy pockets, more like. The man's a shark. With sharp teeth, too. He knew that bear was worth a lot more money than the seventy-five quid he offered you for it. He was spinning you a line, Joel, hoping you'd sell Horace cheaply to him. I'm glad you took my advice and didn't.' He opened a shallow drawer and pulled out a sealed pack of drawing paper. 'Have you told your parents what happened on Friday?'

I shook my head.

'Well, I think you should. Sounds to me as if Horace might be worth insuring. I was talking to my partner about it yesterday and she reckons you should take him to that bear shop in town and see about getting him properly valued. You know the one I mean? Near the library? Lucan's?'

'I think so, yes.'

'Wouldn't hurt to pop him in there and ask. You never know, you could be cuddling a small furry fortune. That'd be a nice surprise for Mum and Dad, wouldn't it?' He split the paper pack open with a satisfying crack, but the look on his face didn't complement the sound. 'You all right, Joel? You look a little edgy.'

'I'm OK,' I whispered.

But I wasn't and he knew it. Pushing the pack aside, he came over and perched on the corner of his desk, one cowboy-booted foot on the floor, the other one swinging free. 'You seemed to give a start when I mentioned Mum and Dad. Is everything all right at home?'

I glanced at the clock. Twenty minutes to the bell. No excuse for a hasty escape. 'My sister had an accident on Friday,' I said. 'She fell downstairs and broke her leg.'

'Ouch,' he whistled, twirling his foot. 'I broke this ankle once. Painful experience. How's she doing?'

OK. She was OK now. But back then, I'd thought for one moment she was dead. After the fall, she had lain unconscious for several seconds, blood seeping out of a wound to her temple. Dad's life breath had brought her spluttering back. Then the awful crying had begun. Maddie, in pain, squealing and reaching for her shattered leg; Erin, shaking like a frightened doll; Mum, almost hysterical with panic; and me – yes, I was weeping, too – out of confusion more than anything else. It was like the worst nightmare you could possibly imagine. Our house had never known a drama like it.

'She's in plaster,' I said. 'It goes from her toes, right over her knee. It's going to take nearly six weeks to get better.'

He folded his arms and gave a sympathetic nod. 'Where is she? In hospital?'

'She came out last night.'

'Good,' he said, brushing some marks off his jeans. 'Good that she's at home with her family around her. Someone's going to be available – to look after her, I mean?'

'Mum,' I said in a quiet voice.

He nodded. 'She doesn't go out to work, then, your mum?'

And there it was. He'd found the spot. The one thing everyone at home had been avoiding. Mum *couldn't* work now, because someone had to stay home and care for Maddie. No one knew this better than Maddie herself. On her first night back, before she'd gone to sleep, she'd collapsed into tears and sobbed that she was sorry, over and over and over again. And though Mum had reassured her she had nothing whatsoever to be sorry for, we all knew in our hearts that the accident meant more pressure for the family, right at a time when we needed it least. Tough for Maddie. Tough for us all. It made me gag just thinking about it.

'Got maths,' I said. I snatched up my bag and headed for the door. 'See you later, sir. Bye.'

'Joel?' His voice tried to claw me back. But there were dozens of probing questions there and I knew I couldn't face a single one. I ran from the art room, straight through the library, down past the gym and into the toilets. And there, in a quiet cubicle, I vomited. I yakked up all that was wrong in my life. And that included Horace and whatever he was worth.

On the way out, I met Roopindar. Of all the people whom fate could have thrown together then, it had to pick on me and her. We jerked to a halt in front of one another. 'Joel, you look terrible.'

Cheers, Roopindar. I closed my eyes.

'I don't mean . . . in looks. Upset, you know?'

'Got a lesson,' I said, brushing past her shoulder.

I thought I'd got away, but her heels began to clatter, and the next thing I knew she had run round in front of me and boldly stopped me with a hand to my chest. 'You've got ten minutes before the next lesson. What's the matter? What's wrong?'

I stared at her hand.

She blushed and let it fall.

As I started to move away, she opened up again. 'Hey, do you wanna sit outside for a bit?'

The absurdity of it made me pause.

She nodded at an empty bench in the yard. 'You don't have to. I'll go away if you like.'

She took a chance then and opened the outside door. The rush of air felt clean and cool on my skin. I moved towards it, not really knowing why. Roopindar stepped out and sat on the bench, sliding along it to the far end. She straightened her skirt and tucked her hands under her bum. I slouched down beside her, legs spread-eagled, chin slumped firmly into my chest. For a while all we did was soak up the sunshine. Then she found a way into my thoughts: 'Did your mum like the thimble?'

For Roopindar, this was just an innocent question, a 'safe' way of getting the pair of us talking. But for me, it was like a punch in the guts. In all the drama on Friday afternoon, Mum's birthday had passed by virtually unnoticed. But I *had* remembered to give her the thimble, while Dad and Maddie were down at Casualty. She'd held it in her hand for the next two hours as if it was some kind of good luck charm. It was now on the mantelpiece, in the front room. It hadn't made its way into the set just yet.

Roopindar stretched out a slim blue leg, the sheen of her school tights glistening on her shin. 'Shall I tell you what the writing means?'

I looked at her blankly. 'I thought it was a pattern.'

'It's Punjabi,' she laughed, with a flash of her teeth. 'My parents taught me it, when I was little. They think it's good for me and Rajinder – he's my brother – to know about our "cultural heritage". The words mean "wealth and happiness" or something like that.' She turned, smiling, only to say, 'It's not working, though, is it?'

I avoided the question and asked one of her. 'Did you see who put it on the stall?'

A second went by. She traced a crack in the flagstones with her toes. 'Me. I put it there before the sale opened. I painted it, too, to make it look pretty. My uncle got it for me; it was the only one he had. Laura was keeping it till you turned up. No one else would have taken it, honest.'

Now I was mega-confused. 'Why didn't you just give it to me?'

'Don't know,' she whispered, tilting her head. Her face disappeared behind her hair. 'Scared, I s'pose. Didn't know what you'd think of me after Dad went and showed me up like that. So I thought, y'know, I'd play it cool.' She leaned forward, knocking her knees together. 'I'm dead sorry about the park. It was Laura's idea. She knows I like you. She thought if she put us together like that we might end up as friends, that's all. I didn't want a date or anything heavy; Mum and Dad wouldn't allow that, anyway. Dumb move, really. How to impress a boy, not.'

Now it was my turn to be tracing flagstones. I rubbed out a weed with the lip of my shoe while I wondered how to reply to her. The scary thing was, I wanted to tell her she was wrong about the 'not'; I *had* been impressed with her, especially how she'd dressed. I hadn't stopped thinking about that night. Or about her. Me and her. Picking at the point of my tie I said, 'I've never been out with anyone before.'

'Me neither,' she said, sounding nervous but hopeful. 'Do you want to, then? Go out, I mean?'

I lifted my shoulders. 'What do we have to do?'

We'll just, y'know, hang out, like mates. Like you do with Kenny. It's just . . . I dunno, different.'

'Do I have to snog you?'

'Joel!' She looked a little shocked by that. 'Going out together isn't just about snogging! It's about being happy in someone else's company.' She moved her foot sideways and let it touch mine. 'If it's a proper friendship, it means you can trust the other person and tell them things . . . things that might be troubling you, yeah?' Her eyebrows lifted. This was my cue.

So I told her. Everything. About Maddie. About Horace – and the charity shop. About Mum and Dad's problems. About yakking in the loo. All of it.

'Wow,' she said, hunching her shoulders forward. 'Think I'd have yakked too. Or cried. Or both. That's gross about your sister. But maybe you can help your mum and dad, eh?'

'How?'

'If the bear's worth loads of dosh, you could sell it and help your dad's business, couldn't you?'

'I don't want to sell him.'

'Not even for your family?'

I lifted my foot and tightened a lace. 'He's falling apart. He can't be worth *that* much.'

'Dunno. That Cholmondeley bloke wanted him.'

True. She had a point there. He'd wanted Horace badly. It kind of gave me the chills.

'I reckon Reynolds is right,' said Roo. 'Won't cost you anything to check it out at Lucan's. I'd be going mental if I was you. Imagine it: buying

something for fifty pence that might be worth
. . . five hundred quid! My uncle would think
that was *really* good business.' She laughed and
nudged the heel of my shoe. 'Will you buy me
an ice-cream when you're rich? Double scoop,
with a flake? Don't care if Percy stirs it with *both*
his feet.'

I laughed and my shoulder pressed against
hers.

She turned so red I could almost feel the heat.
I looked sideways at her. She did the same to
me. 'No snogging, OK?'

'OK,' I said.

She hooked my finger and squeezed it softly.

It was weird. I had a girl *friend* for the first
time ever.

Roopindar Seehra.

And it felt all right.

CHAPTER TEN

'It's not fair, that's all,' Kenny was moaning as we stepped off the bus at the stop near the market and started to weave through the Saturday shoppers. 'You've got Roopindar. Why can't I ask Maddie?'

''Cos she likes . . . real lads!' I said, switching Horace to my opposite hand. I had him in a plain white carrier bag. We were taking him to Lucan's, to try to get him valued. 'You're not old enough for Maddie. And anyway, she's always slagging you off. I think a girl has to actually *like* you, Kenny, before she'll agree to go out with you. Try Erin. She thinks you're cute.'

'Oh yeah, dead comic. Ha.'

We skipped between the market stalls and crossed the road. I thought the brisk pace might shake Kenny off the subject, but still he wouldn't let up: 'Can't I just come round and see her? Must be dead boring, stuck in bed all day with your leg wrapped up like a . . . like a tree trunk.'

We passed a dustcart smelling of rotting fruit.

Over the whine of its jaws I shouted, 'She's got her TV and her books and her music and her mobile. Her mates are texting her all the time.'

'Cool. You got her number?'

'No way. She'd kill me.'

He span away, banging his fists against his temples. 'Invite me for tea then. It's been ages. Come on.'

We turned a corner and swept down Main Street, past all the usual high-street stores. 'I *can't*, Kenny. Mum and Dad are dead touchy right now. They cancelled our holiday yesterday. We were s'posed to be going camping in France.'

'So?'

'So they're ecstatically happy, *not*. It's just best that you don't come round for a bit.'

He kicked a burger tray across the pavement and sighed. 'Did you give her my card?'

The card. Drat. I'd been hoping he wouldn't ask about the card. 'Erm, yeah.'

'Did she like it?'

'Must do. She keeps it right by the side of her bed.'

She was using it as a coaster, but I couldn't tell him that. He'd spent hours at school in the art room, making it. When you flipped it open, the words GET WELL, MADDIE were supposed to spring out in joined-up letters. But the words had stayed trapped in the fold of the card and

she'd tossed it to the floor in complete irri-
tation, beating her duvet in a furious huff. I'd
rescued it from death-by-fluff under the
wardrobe and demonstrated how it was
supposed to work. All she'd done was pull a
Year Nine sneer, slam it face down on her
bedside table and grind a soup mug onto it.
Stuffed.

Things were bad with Maddie those first few
days. No matter how we tried to lift her spirits,
she hung weights from them and pulled them
down again. It wasn't only Kenny she was
taking it out on. The slightest little things would
get her riled. If a spider crawled across the
ceiling above her, she'd demand that someone
come in and move it. Not because she was afraid
of spiders (or 'quentins' as she called them, after
the actor Quentin 'Tarantulino') but simply
because it was up there, *leering*, and she couldn't
do a single thing about it. Once you'd done her
bidding, you were instantly dismissed. Only
Mum was allowed to stay with her. Only Mum
was allowed to help her to the bathroom or get
her undressed or wiggle her toes to keep her
circulation going. It was hurting Erin and
annoying me. She wouldn't even let me draw
on her cast. *'No one touches my leg'*, she'd moan,
waving a crutch to show she meant it. Talk
about moody. Talk about girly. I felt for her; she

was my sister after all. But I only went to see her if an errand was required. If Kenny had set one foot in that room, he'd have been turned to stone by her scowl.

'Joel, wait, can we just go in here?'

We slowed to a halt outside the old library.

'I need to swap these.' From his jacket, Kenny pulled out half a dozen books. Young readers. For kids of six or seven. 'They're for Jess,' he said. Jessie was his sister. She was just a little kid and she suffered from asthma. He didn't talk about her all that much.

'OK, but hurry up.'

He sprang up the steps and opened the doors. The librarian at the desk seemed to know him pretty well. While she was scanning books off the system, she smiled and chattered, 'Hello, Kenny, how are you this week? I managed to reserve that *Paddington* you wanted. Pick it up from the issue desk on your way out.'

'Thanks,' he said and nudged through the turnstile.

Bewildered, I asked him, 'Do you come in here a lot?'

'Loads,' he said, bombing off towards the children's section. He pointed proudly to the junior fiction shelves. 'I've read nearly half of those to Jess.'

I had to shake my head. You think you know

everything about your mate, then he clouts your brain with a corker like that. 'You *read* to your sister?'

'She's dyslexic,' he muttered.

'You never told me that.'

'You never asked me,' he said and bent down to scour the shelves like a pro. Within five minutes he'd made his selections and we were beeping our way through the issue desk. He put his six new books inside his jacket, zipped up and said, 'Let's see about Horace.'

Lucan's was a tiny dot of a place. It was on the end of a row of terraced houses that had all been converted into shops. The outside walls were painted pink, so you couldn't miss it from outer space, never mind our local high street. The small bay window was filled with bears. Some dressed, some not. All shapes and sizes. On tiered stands draped with ribbons and lace. I half-expected Horace to poke his snout above the carrier, twizzle his head like a battleship gun turret and have a good look round, the way dogs do when they sense more of their kind. (He didn't, of course.)

'We going in then?' Kenny asked nervously.

I tightened my grip on the handles of the bag, nodded once and pushed the door open. A bell tinkled, announcing our presence. A bloke of about forty, with a droopy grey moustache and his hair pulled back in a tight little pony-tail, looked up from behind a pine chest of drawers he was using as a counter. He was dumpy and looked like he'd eaten a bear. A tug of war team could not have buttoned his waistcoat. He had his shirt sleeves rolled back almost to his armpits and a faint smell of shower gel was rising off him. In his lap was a bear, a lot smaller and a whole lot tidier than Horace. He was brushing its ears with what looked like a toothbrush, making the fur stand up in spikes.

'Good morning,' he said in a wheezy sort of voice. 'What might I do for you?'

I glanced to my left. On the far wall was a large Welsh dresser, studded with bears and a few china dolls. I was hoping to see a bear like Horace that I could point to and ask, 'How much for that?' But just like on the net, not a single teddy came close to mine. I met the man's eyes and my mouth went dry. I managed to splutter, 'Are you Mr Lucan?'

'I am. Larry, not Lord,' he said. It was obviously a joke, but I didn't get it. He glanced at my bag. Horace's big ears were sticking out above it. Mr Lucan – Larry – raised an eyebrow. 'Is that a WB you've got in there?'

'What?' said Kenny.

'He means a Horace,' I said, impressed by Mr Lucan's guesswork. 'How did you know?'

He sat the toothbrushed bear on a glittering gift box and swung his chair right round to face us. 'The ears,' he confided, laying his jewelled hands flat against his thighs. He wore lots of chunky rings and a silver bracelet. In the fuzz of his chest, a St Christopher medallion glinted under the halogen spotlights. 'William B. Horace, the man who first made them, had very small ears. He was bullied about it throughout his childhood. So he made his bears with huge great flaps. It's impossible to miss a WB. May I see him? I take it you've brought him here to show me?' He cleared some space on the counter in front of us.

I took Horace out and plonked him down.

Almost immediately, a look of wonder spread across Larry Lucan's face. He picked Horace up like a new-born baby, wincing as the loose arm tried to flap away and a small amount of stuffing puffed out of the hole. He moved the arm carefully after that, pinning it firmly with his right hand so that no more stitches could rip or tear. Clicking his fingers at a tray by the till, he asked me to pass him a small viewing lens. He squinted through it at Horace's label.

'Well, boys, this is quite a find.'

'What can you see?' I shifted forward.

'Nineteen twenty-one,' he said proudly.

'Is that when he was made?'

'Mmm, in the original factory, in Withenshaw – if this label is to be believed. It certainly *looks* genuine. Just a moment, let me test his eyes.' Putting the lens aside, he stuck out his tongue and licked Horace's eyes.

'Ugh,' went Kenny, reeling back. 'What'd you do that for?'

'Old-fashioned test,' Mr Lucan said. 'They feel cold, which means they're made of glass, not plastic, which means they're probably his original eyes, which means he's almost certainly genuine.' He positioned Horace upright on the counter again, tilting his chin like a judge checking out a dog at Crufts. 'Handsome, isn't he?'

'He's manky,' said Kenny.

Mr Lucan frowned. 'I'll grant you he's not been well looked after. But that doesn't change his basic demeanour. With bears, it's all in the stare, you see. That's what they go for, the true collectors. You can't beat a bear with a decent *look*.' He reached for a catalogue on a shelf behind him, flicked through it quickly and folded back a page. 'There, that's a classic twenties Horace. Not quite the same as yours, but pretty comparable. That's what he would have looked like when he was new.'

'Wow,' went Kenny. Even he was impressed. The bear in the picture had fluffy golden fur and perfectly jointed arms and legs. He was like . . . son of Horace, after the car wash.

'How do I get mine like that?' I asked.

'You don't,' said Mr Lucan, wagging a finger. 'You mustn't go near him with any kind of domestic cleaning material; you'll ruin him if you do.'

'Can't we just chuck him in the washing machine?' asked Kenny.

Mr Lucan shuddered with horror. 'That would be tantamount to teddy bear murder. Restoring old bears is a specialist business. He needs to be cleaned professionally, millimetre by millimetre. It won't be cheap, either. To clean and repair a bear like him, in his battered state, is going to set you back a few hundred pounds.'

'What?!' screeched Kenny.

Mr Lucan closed his eyes. His veiny lids fluttered like a pair of butterflies. 'It would be an investment,' he explained patiently. 'If the bear is groomed, his value will increase – not a great deal, but enough to make the layout worth your while.'

I felt a gnawing in my stomach then and had to ask, 'How much is he worth? Do you know?'

Mr Lucan pursed his lips. 'Well, I'm not an expert with bears of this age – you don't see many of them around these days – but I was at an auction a few months ago where a Horace like this was put under the hammer, and it went for around eight thousand pounds.'

A trail of slobber dribbled down Kenny's chin.

'And that was a thirties bear,' said Mr Lucan. 'This old boy's a good ten years older. It's a shame I can't read his series number – that would be a real advantage in pricing him. I can just make out the first two numerals, but the others are slightly soiled.'

'What's . . . ?'

'A series number?' he guessed.

I nodded. I could hardly move my tongue. That figure was still tumbling through my mind. One eight, three zeros. *Ching. Ching. Ching.* Not tens. Not hundreds. *Thousands* of pounds.

He put the catalogue aside and turned Horace towards us. 'During the early years, before the days of mass-production, it was fashionable for the Horace company to make their bears in batches of twenty. They were hand-stitched, of course, and each batch was labelled with a series number. When a set was complete, the makers would change the design very slightly and give the next set of twenty a longer snout or extra stitching around the nose, just a little something to differentiate them from other batches.'

He paused, clearly expecting a comment, but we were both too gobsmacked to interrupt.

'It made them more collectable,' Mr Lucan went on. 'That zero one two you see on his label means that your fellow is number twelve in an exclusive club of twenty. In other words, there are or were only another nineteen bears in existence who look exactly like him. Some series are more sought after than others. If we can pin his grouping down it will be much easier to give you an idea of just how popular he's going to be. As it happens, I know someone who might be able to help you with that, a regular customer who's spent half his life in the company of these bears. Lovely old gent. Pops in all the time. You probably know him in a roundabout way. Mr Arnold?'

We shook our heads.

'Percy Arnold,' he hinted. 'I'm sure you've eaten his famous ice-cream.'

Kenny sat up smartly. 'What, the bloke who—?'

'Kenny,' I hissed, giving him a smack. This wasn't the time to be talking about stirring vanilla with your feet.

'Percy's, that's right,' Mr Lucan beamed. 'Very wealthy man. Lives in that big house on top of Clumber Hill. Do you know it?'

We ought to. We'd nicked conkers from the

grounds on many an autumn night. That was where the man who made Percy's lived?

'He's an expert on old-fashioned bears like this. He'll probably fall in love with it the moment he sees it; wouldn't surprise me if he didn't want to buy it off you. I'll give him a ring. See if he's interested. How's that?'

'Cool,' said Kenny. '*Eight thousand,*' he mouthed with a loopy grin.

Mr Lucan pushed Horace back towards me. 'You're a lucky young man to be in possession of a bear like this, but can I offer you a word of advice? Try not to cuddle him or play with him too much. These bears are not toys. They were made to be admired, loved from a distance. The more damaged he becomes, the more his value drops. He's been through the wars a bit, this chap. Looks like he'd appreciate a bit of a rest.' He touched a finger to Horace's snout, then tapped a small wad of Lucan's notepaper. 'Write your telephone number on this pad. I'll call you when I've made a few enquiries.'

CHAPTER ELEVEN

It was that same morning that Mum and Dad received their third big blow.

Just a week after Dad had lost his client, and Maddie's leg had snapped at the bottom of the stairs, a letter came from Dad's insurance company. I learned about this from Erin, of course, who'd been in the kitchen when he'd knifed it open. He'd groaned, 'Oh, Jesus, that's all we need.' And the letter had gone at arm's length to Mum, who'd sunk into a chair with a hand across her mouth. Erin had begged them to tell her what it meant. But this time they'd sent her out of the room and the door to the kitchen was firmly closed. There had been no shouting, no raised voices. But through the upturned glass on the floor of her room, Erin claimed to have heard the words, 'Not the house?' I didn't know what it meant. Mum and Dad weren't saying. We weren't asking. And this time there was no big family meet.

But to say that the atmosphere was gloomy

after that would be like admitting that dungeons aren't cosy. You could feel the disaster cloud out in the road. Everything *seemed* to be going on as normal. But Dad was never there, even when he was at home, and Mum had turned into this perfect machine, this robot mother that packed us off efficiently to school in the mornings and organized tea for us when we returned. These were the things she'd always done. But now there was this prickly sort of force field around her, and a sharpness on her tongue if you questioned anything. Her dark brown eyes were like old buttons, dull and staring, never changing size. My mum, the person I loved most of all in the world, was turning into a joyless zombie.

And all the while I had the means to reverse it.

I'd played this through lots of times in my head. It would have been so cool to go to them and say, 'Mum, Dad, I'm giving you Horace. Hey, guess what? He's worth *this* much.' Then watch their faces swell with surprise, and possibly even pride, and hopefully relief. But something was always holding me back. Some nagging doubt that I couldn't shake off or dampen down. Several times that week I had nightmares about it. I would dream that my ears had turned into gargoyles, spitting and laughing inside my head, warning me that if I talked about Horace a mountain of trouble was waiting to fall.

But I'd known that the moment we'd left Mr Lucan's. I'd looked at Kenny, and he at me, and we both knew the situation had changed. We were no longer travelling with a cuddly toy; we were Hadleigh and Jones, charity shop robbers, with a heavy wad of banknotes in our carrier, cunningly disguised as a straw-coloured bear. I had nicked eight thousand quid's worth of teddy. Butterflies were not so much fluttering inside me as riding the wall of death in my stomach. If Mum and Dad learned the truth of what I'd done, some serious questions would have to be faced. It was crazy. All I'd wanted was a project for art. Now I felt like a suspect on the run.

I ran to the art room first, of course, hoping I could talk it through with Mr Reynolds. I was going to confess my 'sin' to him, because that was how the gargoyles saw it, I knew. But Mr Reynolds had the flu and was missing all week. So I decided I would wait, not do anything silly, and in the meantime take Mr Lucan's advice and keep Horace safely out of harm's way. That's why I put him on my wardrobe top. And that's why Erin and I fell out – and Mum got to hear about Roopindar.

'Why?!' moaned Erin, stamping a foot.

'Because . . . I'm drawing him from a different angle!'

'I'll put him back like he was before.'

'No.'

'I can memorize how he was sitting.'

'No.'

'I can. Honestly.'

'Erin, I've told you! He's staying on top of the wardrobe, OK?'

'No! Bring him down. I want to cuddle him!'

'You can't.'

'Joel, don't be so mean!'

'Oh, will you two please SHUT UP?!' Maddie's voice rang out from the room next to mine, followed by Mum's as she swept up the stairs.

'What's going on?'

Erin rushed to the landing. 'I want to cuddle Horace and Joel won't let me.'

Mum sighed and put the heel of her palm to her head. 'Give her the bear, Joel.'

'No,' I said.

Mum's face hardened into a frown. 'I beg your pardon?'

'Burn it. It's driving me mental,' Maddie shouted. 'They're always going on about that stupid bear.'

'Maddie, be quiet,' Mum shouted back. 'What's your problem, Joel?'

'I'm drawing him,' I said. 'I don't want him moved.'

'He's never said that before,' griped Erin. 'And what's the point of drawing him on top of the wardrobe? You can hardly even *see* him up there. I'm going to get him down.'

I grabbed her shoulder as she turned.

'Get off!' she yelped, flailing an arm.

'You're not going to play with him!'

'I am!'

'You're not!'

'Oh, stop it! For goodness' sake!' yelled Mum. 'Don't you think things are bad enough without you lot squabbling amongst yourselves? Joel, stop acting soft. Give Erin the bear and be done with it.'

'No.'

Mum looked at me as if I'd been swapped at birth. 'What on earth is the matter with you?'

'It's his hormones,' Maddie shouted, and that seemed to give Erin the push she needed.

'Move!' she cried, trying to wrestle me aside. 'I s'pose you don't care about *me* any more. Just 'cos you've got a girlfriend now!'

That stopped the argument dead.

'Girlfriend?' Mum shook her head, confused.

I glared at Erin. She kept her face down and closed up like a flower. She knew she'd done wrong. Roopindar was supposed to be our biggest secret. My sister, my ally, the quiet one, had betrayed me.

'Joel's got a *girlfriend*?!' Maddie squeaked loudly. *Her* zest for life had suddenly returned. 'Aw, that's gross. Come and talk in here, where I can see you. Mum, what's he look like? Has he gone ruby?'

Yes, he had. Ruby with anger. 'I'm going out,' I barked at Mum. And to Erin: 'Don't you *dare* move Horace, *ever again*!'

She turned away, tearstruck, and picked at the wall.

As I clumped down the stairs, I glanced back at Mum. And I don't know how it happened, but this hiss came rising from the back of my throat and I snapped at her nastily: 'You don't have to *stare*. I'm only going to *Kenny's*.'

Her look became one of 'what have I lost?' and neither she nor Erin said a single word. The last word in our house was always Maddie's, anyway.

'Oh, tell me what's happening. Someone? *Please?* I HATE having a broken leg.'

CHAPTER TWELVE

I didn't go to Kenny's. I went to Roopindar's.
I'd been doing this every night for a week,
calling round at her house after tea, then walking
her down to the park to meet her mates. Kenny
and Laura, despite their 'split', were generally
there as well. But that night it rained down
gargoyle spit. The skies turned evil and I needed
the umbrella of bricks and mortar. When Mrs
Seehra opened the door, I was under the tent of
my denim jacket. She said something in Punjabi
and hauled me inside. Towels were produced.
A hot drink ordered. Roopindar, like her mum,
started bleating about chills. Her dad said, 'The
boy is not a puppy dog; rain won't hurt him.'
And he called me into their large front room.
He'd pushed back all the seating and was
building something from a flat-pack box. He
beckoned me over and showed me the diagram.

'Joel, cast your eye upon this.'

I took it and turned it the right way up.

'These mysterious pieces of beech must be
transformed into a handsome bookshelf within

the hour or my wife will have me sleeping in the garage tonight. Can you find cam bolt D, times four? They are to be introduced to counter-sunk holes on side panels A, times two, and locked in place with a half twist of this.' He held up a small yellow screwdriver.

'Dad, he's come to see me, remember?' Roopindar walked in and plonked a cup of tea on the mantelpiece for me, in between a framed photo of her parents' wedding and one of several wooden elephants dotted about the room. 'He doesn't want to build a stupid bookshelf.'

Her father, switching languages, ticked her off.

Roopindar closed her hands and apologized to him. 'It's good Sikh practice to be helpful,' she explained.

'Indeed,' said her father, stroking his beard. 'Besides, if I allowed you to go to your room with Joel, who knows what shenanigans might occur.'

'Da-ad!' Roopindar's mouth fell open like a bucket.

'Shenanigans?' I asked.

'Cam bolt D,' he reminded me quietly.

I split a pack of screws and started to look.

Huffing loudly, Roopindar sank down on the edge of the sofa. It was a plush green leather one with matching chairs; you could have seated half a football team on it. Unlike us, the Seehra family were not short of money. Their house was enormous and their garden even bigger; it tumbled away down a long grassy slope, ending at the bottom at the Union Canal. They didn't have a boat, but they did possess pretty much everything else: two bathrooms (I knew because I'd used them both); two cars and a caravan on the drive; a kitchen so large you could have held the next school disco in it; window blinds that closed at the touch of a button; carpets that felt like jelly underfoot; a Siamese cat called Soni; and my favourite thing of all, a pond most people would call a small ocean, so crammed with white and orange carp that herons came across two counties to steal them.

Roopindar, of course, had everything she needed. Her uncle worked in the clothing trade and brought her something new from his warehouse every week. Apart from at school, I never saw Roo in the same thing twice. Tonight she was wearing a v-necked top and a pair of black trousers that flared at the ankles, stitched with a kind of seahorse motif. Her hair was tied back in a high pony-tail and for once I could see her small, cute ears. Neat and pretty, that's what she was. A smart, rich girl who could have been a total pain in the bum, but never once acted that way with me. In the space of a week, I'd grown to know what it could be like to miss her. We still hadn't kissed, but I'd thought about it – lots. (I'd practised alone on the back of my hand.)

Checking to see that her father wasn't looking, she leaned forward and whispered, 'Have you heard from Mr Lucan yet?' She knew the whole story of Horace by now. Her father, Mr Seehra, didn't.

'Who is Mr Lucan?' he enquired straight away.

'Oh, Dad! You've got ears like Ramu!' she sparked, pointing to one of the elephant carvings. 'You're not s'posed to be listening. I was talking to Joel. It's none of your business.'

'Everything you do is my business,' he warned her, burbling away to the tape of prayers playing continuously in the background. This, like the giddy smell of incense, was a constant feature of the Seehra household. 'Bolts?' he asked.

I handed him the ones I'd checked against the diagram and showed him where I thought they should fit.

'Ah, true genius,' he beamed. 'Roopindar, you must stay a friend to this boy. He understands shelving. A very worthy skill. Now, who is Mr Lucan?'

Roopindar put the heels of her hands to her temples, loosening a bangle down her arm. She looked good like this, bristling slightly, her long reedy eyebrows as straight as swords. 'It's OK,' she said, catching sight of my wary expression, 'you can tell him about Horace. He won't *say* anything. He's just being Dad, that's all.' She put the flat of one sandal against his bum and pushed him towards the widescreen TV.

'Mr Lucan is also called Horace?' he asked.

'No!' Roo called, in complete exasperation.

To spare her nerves I began to tell the story, leaving out the bit about the charity-shop skip and pausing at the point of Mr Lucan's valuation.

'Tell him how much,' Roopindar jabbered eagerly, her sandal backs flapping against her heels. 'Eight thousand!' she blurted, before I could speak.

Mr Seehra stopped saying his prayers. 'Then you should *definitely* stick with this boy. Eight thousand pounds could buy a lot of shelving. Joel, if your wealth hasn't gone to your head, help me to lay this beast on its front.'

We each took an end and tipped the shelves over. The outer frame was assembled by now. To make up the back, we had to hammer on a hardboard panel. Mr Seehra put it in position. As we spread the panel pins around the four sides, Roo asked, 'What do you think he should do with Horace, Dad?'

Her father pondered a moment. His eyes, already set back in their sockets, seemed to glide deeper into his head. 'This Horace is a bear for collectors, yes?'

'Yes,' I said.

'And you found it in a shop where people make donations?'

Roo crossed her arms. 'What are you getting at, Dad?'

Her father rolled a pin between his fingers. He had large, strong hands. They looked too clumsy for this kind of work. I held my breath as he picked up the hammer. 'I am merely asking myself who would put a bear like that in such a shop.'

Me and Roopindar exchanged a glance.

'What difference does it make?' she asked.

Her father chattered something in Punjabi again and bobbed his head from side to side. 'Maybe the person making this donation hoped that the charity would benefit from the sale of the bear.'

With a bang that made me and all the loose pins jump, he drove the first one safely home. He didn't yelp with pain or sit back bruised. Not so ham-handed after all.

Roopindar wiggled her razor-straight nose. 'Dad, no one gives a charity shop eight thousand quid. Anyway, the person who left him would have sold Horace first, then given them the money, wouldn't they?'

Her father conceded a nod. 'That would be the usual way, I agree. But what if this person wished to be anonymous? Not everyone likes to take pride from what they give. Then there is the other possibility, of course.'

'What's that?' I asked, interested but nervous.

He hammered in another pin before replying. 'That whoever owned the bear did not know its worth – and gave it away, unaware they could have sold it.'

'Tough,' said Roo, jumping in right away. 'It's Joel's bear now.' She smiled at me as if to say, *'Finders keepers.'*

But her dad had a point; two points, in fact. What if he was right about a secretive donor and the charity had lost eight thousand pounds – water for Africa, that sort of thing? Or what if the person who'd given Horace up had been a confused old pensioner or something, living on their own, not knowing that the raggy bear they'd chucked on the scrap heap could have paid the bills for years and years?

Another pin went in. My head jerked up.

'Smile. You're going to be rich,' said Roo.

I shook my head. 'I'm not going to sell him.'

Mr Seehra flicked me a look: a mix of curiosity and quiet respect.

Roopindar toyed with a wisp of her hair. 'But I thought—'

'Will you help me?' I blurted, before she could spill about the family problems. I was pretty sure that was where her sentence was heading, and I didn't want her father to know about that.

'Help you? With what?'

I looked at her dad, chewing on a pin. Thanks to him, my brain had stopped spinning for a moment. Now I knew what had troubled me in my dreams: Horace's homesick look. The bear wasn't mine; he never really had been. I'd saved him from the crusher, paid his fifty pence 'ransom'. But that didn't grant me the right to own him or trade him in for a bagful of money. I'd feel guilty for the rest of my life if I did. So I told Roopindar what I planned to do. 'I'm going to try and find him – or her, maybe.'

'Who?' she replied, looking even more mystified.

'Whoever had Horace before me,' I said.

CHAPTER THIRTEEN

Roopindar did a perfect Maddie expression: eyes big, mouth wide, face totally bemused. 'You're going to try and find the original owner?'

I shrugged. It seemed a good idea to me.

'But why?' she bleated. 'That doesn't make sense. That way you'll lose Horace – *and* the money.'

Mr Seehra wagged his screwdriver at me. 'For once, I agree with my headstrong daughter. What you're proposing is a noble gesture, Joel, and I, for one, admire you for it. But when I raised the question of who donated the bear, I was merely being curious, not trying to prick your conscience. Roopindar is right. If you made this purchase in good faith, even at the modest price of fifty pence, legally the bear belongs to you and no one can make a claim on it. You have no obligation to demonstrate such honour.'

He turned away to drive another pin into the shelves.

Roopindar blew a sigh and looked at me again. But now the surprise and bewilderment had gone and uncertainty was clouding her chocolate-coloured eyes. I knew what she was thinking: I hadn't made a purchase, and not in good faith; legally the bear did *not* belong to me. The gremlin of guilt was upon me again. I made a small face and she shrugged as if to say, 'It doesn't matter, does it? Who's going to know?'

But when her dad raised his head again *he* seemed to know. He saw my gaze plummet deep into the shadows and noticed straight away that Roopindar was anxiously twiddling her thumb ring. 'Daughter, you are nervous,' he said to her idly. 'I am wondering why *that* can be?'

To her credit, Roopindar made a brilliant recovery. 'I'm just disappointed with Joel, Daddy-ji. He promised he would buy me an ice-cream castle – when he was rich from the sale of Horace.'

Clever. Her father was instantly fooled. 'Ice-cream, bah. Bad for the figure.' He gave his substantial paunch a slap. As if he'd called a genie out of its bottle, Mrs Seehra emerged from the steaming kitchen, carrying a tray of sweet-smelling food.

'Joel, you'll have a little snack?' she asked, peering at me over her round black glasses. She was very small, even to a boy of my age. Her head seemed permanently tilted back.

I looked at the tray. On it was a plate of crackling samosas, a bowl of savoury nuts and beans and a big dish of *mattar*: deep-fried green peas mixed with chilli. I liked them best. They stripped the skin off your tonsils, but once you'd had a few you couldn't stop eating them. 'Thanks,' I said, and took a small handful.

'It's stopped raining,' Roo said. 'Come on, let's go out.'

Her father batted a hand. 'The boy is eating. Let him enjoy our hospitality. Besides, it's time for your homework, I think.'

Roopindar tutted and frowned at the clock.

I took the hint and told them I ought to be going.

'Have something for the journey,' Mr Seehra said, flapping his hammer towards the tray.

Just to be polite I took a samosa and ate it on my way to the hall.

Roopindar came to show me out. 'Are you serious about finding Horace's owner?'

I nodded, losing pastry crumbs down my fleece.

'But what about your mum and dad? I thought you were going to sell him to help them?'

'Can't,' I said, keeping my voice as low as I could, wary that her parents might overhear. 'It's not right, is it, if he doesn't belong to me?'

She crossed her arms and looked away, frowning.

'I don't want to lose Horace, really,' I said. 'I know it's uncool, but I like him; he's neat. But if he's worth as much as Mr Lucan says, we ought to try and find out who he belongs to and give them the chance to take him back. That's what you'd do if you found someone's purse on the pavement, wouldn't you?'

She extended her gaze a little further up the stairs, to a picture of a smiling Guru, and shrugged. 'How, though? How're you gonna track the owner down? That's like . . . mission impossible, yeah?'

I'd already thought about that. In theory, the process was simple. I would go back to the charity shop and ask the woman, Doris, if she could remember who'd brought Horace in. If the donor was someone fairly local, someone who came to the shop quite often, Doris might know them or remember their face and could collar them the next time they came through the door. I told Roo this. She immediately shook her head.

'Can't, you twonk, they'll know you nicked him.'

Good point. She was smart, this girl. 'Then . . . I'll say I want a bear like the one they had and I wondered if the person who'd brought

Horace in might have another one like him. Easy.'

'Hmm,' she went. She didn't look convinced.

'Anyway, I'm not gonna do it till I've seen Percy Arnold. I want to make doubly sure that Horace is worth eight thousand pounds. Are you gonna come with me?'

She dragged her pony-tail over her shoulder, stroking it like the tail of a cat. 'You want me to visit a millionaire with you?'

'Yeah.'

'Hmm. Cool date! You're on!' She flashed a big grin and was about to say more, but in the lounge her parents were beginning to stir. 'Time to go,' she said, and wiped a crumb off my mouth.

It was the first time she'd ever touched my lips. I looked into her eyes and she into mine. Slowly, our heads began to tilt . . .

. . . then the door to the front room opened and her father's mammoth presence filled it.

'See you tomorrow!' we both said loudly, and in a whoosh we had gone our separate ways, just a shower of samosa crumbs left on the carpet and the jangle of a cowbell on the firmly closed door.

I was still smirking from ear to ear when I burst into the kitchen at Castle Doom. I came in through the back way across the wet lawn – and found Dad alone at the kitchen table. He wasn't in his usual seat. He was facing the door with his back to the hall. It looked as if he'd been waiting for me.

'Joel,' he said. It was a greeting not far short of a reprimand. A sort of 'Hello, son', without a lot of warmth.

'Hi, Dad.' I sat down to untie my trainers. I kept my eyes low. I didn't want to look at him. I'd left the house in anger. He'd know about that.

'Where've you been?' he asked quietly.

'Out.'

'In the rain?'

'Kenny's,' I lied, remembering my outburst. Kenny's. I was s'posed to have gone to Kenny's.

He nodded and picked up a small cork coaster, tumbling it slowly through his fingers. 'That's strange. Kenny rang here twenty minutes ago, wanting to know if you'd meet him in the park. Your mum told him she thought you were out with him already. Obviously you weren't.'

'Well, I changed my mind, OK?' Anger and embarrassment surged up inside me. I hated it when Mum and Dad caught me out like this. I forced off a shoe and started on the other. 'I've got other mates as well as Kenny, you know.'

'So I hear,' he said, his tone not varying. He

was good at this; quietly making us squirm. He dropped the coaster and tapped its centre. 'Your mum was worried. She said you went out in a bit of a sulk. Do you want to tell me about it?'

Of course I didn't! Why did they always ask you that? I turned my head away from him and focused on the door of the washing machine. This was stupid; I didn't want to look at *clothes* going round. But I didn't want to talk about the argument either. I hoped if I played dumb he'd let it go.

He didn't. 'What was all this with Erin?'

My tired gaze panned across the fridge. In the lines of magnetic letters on the door I could see the word TEDDY in reds and blues. Nice one, Erin. Thank you very much. 'She wouldn't listen when I asked her not to move Horace.'

'What was he doing on top of the wardrobe?'

'I was *drawing* him. Why doesn't anyone listen?'

He raised his chin and set his mouth into a line. Although he didn't say it, he was telling me to 'watch it'. 'Erin says she checked every one of your sketch books and there were no new drawings of Horace in them.'

'Well, she shouldn't have!' I cried out, thumping the table. 'She's a nosy little—!'

'Hey,' he snapped, almost pinning me to the wall with the force of the word. This time it *was* a serious warning. 'You don't badmouth your sister, OK? You and Erin have hardly had a cross word in your lives. So why now? What's the big deal with the bear?'

'His arm's coming off. She'll mess him up if she plays with him.'

'Fine. Your mum's good with a needle and thread. She's already offered to repair him once.'

'Dad, you can't just stitch him up. Horace is *old*. You have to be an expert to fix him properly. You don't understand.' I was on my feet now and heading for the door.

'Wait,' he ordered. 'You go when I say.'

Parent power. The ultimate weapon. I slumped against the wall and slammed my hands into my pockets.

His eyes took on a beady, penetrating glare. 'You're right, Joel, I don't understand. I don't understand why my son is being devious, and keeping secrets, and yelling at his family at a time when his family could most do without it. All right, it's your bear to do with as you like. But you apologize to Erin and you explain to her *politely* why you don't want it handled. *And* you say sorry to your mother. Understood?'

'Yes,' I mumbled and rolled off the wall.

'Oh, and one last thing.' He reached out and picked up the coaster again, turning it slowly as he had before. 'You had another phone call, just before Kenny's. A Mr Lucan, from a shop called World of Bears. I told him you were out. He left this message.'

From the pocket of his shirt he pulled a scrap of paper. I took it and read.

Mr Arnold v. keen to value Horace.
2pm, Sunday. At his house.

Dad lifted his gaze. His sharp blue eyes were like two circular panes of glass. He stood the coaster vertical, then let it fall. 'How much is he really worth?' he asked.

CHAPTER FOURTEEN

I told him a half-truth. I said I wasn't sure. I said we'd had this treasure thing at school one night and that this dodgy antiques bloke called Christopher Cholmondeley had offered me seventy-five pounds for Horace and Mr Reynolds had advised me not to accept it and told me to take him to Lucan's instead.

'And?' Dad tapped an inquisitive foot.

'Mr Lucan didn't know his proper value. I have to show him to Mr Arnold.'

'Who's Mr Arnold?'

'That bloke who makes the ice-cream. He knows about bears.'

'*Percy* Arnold? The millionaire? The big thatched cottage on Clumber Hill?'

'Yes.'

Dad pushed a hand into the crown of his hair and gave a dazed little shake of his head. 'You mean, the family's on the verge of—? And you're doing business with—?' He sank forwards onto his elbows, rubbing his temples in a circular motion. 'Is this why you didn't want him moved? Because his value goes down if he loses that arm?'

I shrugged and looked out of the window. It was raining again and the street lights were on.

With a snort of laughter, Dad rose to his feet. 'Well, I'll give you this: you're certainly not short on enterprise, Joel.' He looked me up and down and his mood became serious. 'If you're planning to sell Horace to a man like Percy Arnold, someone should be with you to negotiate properly. An adult. I'd better drive you up there myself.'

'No,' I said urgently. 'I don't want to sell him. I just want to know how much he's worth.'

Now I got one of those extended stares, the kind that meant I hadn't quite given him a good enough reason to believe I should be left to my own devices. So I clawed something useful from the back of my brain: 'Mr Reynolds said we might have to get him insured.'

'Oh, did he?' he said with blunt-edged indifference. 'And perhaps Mr Reynolds would like to pay the premium? What kind of figures are we talking here? Didn't this Lucan bloke give you any idea?'

I shrugged and tried to think how to change the subject. If he pushed me, I'd crack, and I still wasn't sure I wanted him to know that Horace was more than your average teddy. Then the fate fairies came to my rescue. Propped against the door of the microwave was the letter from Dad's insurance company, stamped with the logo and the company name. 'Dad?'

'Anyway, why don't you want to sell it?' he muttered. 'What else were you planning to do with it?'

I ignored him and picked up the letter. 'What's this? Erin said it was about the house.'

Leaning forward, he slid it out of my grasp. 'That's private, for me and your mum to sort out.'

'Is it serious? Have we got to move?'

'Joel . . .' he began, only to cut himself short with a sigh. He looked at the ceiling, as if he were sitting a big exam and the answers to his problems were written in the plaster.

'I'll keep it secret. I promise. Scouts' honour.'

'You weren't in the scouts,' he reminded me pithily, filing the letter into his pocket. He turned to the sink and filled a glass with water. He drank a large mouthful and ditched the rest. 'If I tell you, not a word to the girls. Are we clear?'

'Yes,' I said, and bunched my toes. The kitchen floor suddenly felt cold underfoot.

Arms folded, he leaned back hard against the worktop. 'You're right, the letter is about the house, about our mortgage to be precise. Do you know what a mortgage is?'

'It's when you borrow money to buy a house.'
We'd done it at school once.

'Yes,' he said. 'A loan that has to be repaid, with interest. For the past fourteen years we've been paying regular amounts into an insurance policy, which is supposed to earn enough money to cover the loan we took out to buy this house. In twelve months' time the plan will mature and the bank will demand that we repay what we borrowed, in full. But the insurance policy hasn't done well, which basically means we won't have enough cash to pay the bank off. If something isn't done, we'll be in serious debt. Then we'll have no choice but to sell up and move – to somewhere smaller, perhaps another area. That would break your mother's heart. That's why she's been quiet for the last few days. On top of me losing a chunk of my income, she's now worried that we're going to lose our home.'

Absent-mindedly, I touched the wall. These bricks. I'd lived inside them all my life. How strange would it be not to know them any more? 'What will you do?'

He looked at me quizzically.

'You said that something had to be done.'

He passed a hand across his face, scraping the stubbled hairs darkening his chin. 'I don't know. I need to talk to the accountant. But things aren't going to be easy, Joel. The only way we'll get through is as a family. More than ever, I need us to pull together now. So no more squabbles with your sisters, OK? Which reminds me, Maddie's been asking for you.'

'Maddie? What does she want?'

He pushed away from the worktop and tousled my hair. 'There's only one way to find out.'

She was propped against a cluster of cushions and pillows, with her legs stretched out on the bed, when I arrived. I leaned against the door frame, waiting for an invite, but as usual her gaze was buried in a book and the loud *tish tish* of her mini-disc player meant that her ears were well off limits. I hadn't seen her properly for several days, so it was interesting just to look at her for a second, dressed in the fashion accessories of the moment: a pair of Mum's old cotton pyjamas, sliced to the hip on her broken side, and a 'sock' that resembled a small tea cosy over the exposed part of her foot. Without make-up she looked pale-faced and delicate: younger, less cynical, but just as striking. That was the coolest thing about Maddie: she never had to try to look good, she just did. Even the cut on her forehead had healed, and there was no suggestion that she might be scarred. Her cast, like her face, was completely unblemished (apart from the peel-off label of an apple which I'd stuck near her ankle in a fit of pique and which she either couldn't reach or still hadn't seen). I thought about sneaking in and signing it quickly, but valuing my life, I tapped the door instead. She didn't respond. I waved my hands. Nothing. *OK, Ginger, I'm going in.* On the end of the bed were a pile of magazines. I bounced down, grabbed one and started flipping through it.

'Hey, do you mind?!' She slammed her book down and pulled off her headphones. 'Knock before you come in, OK?'

'I did; you were reading. Ugh, this is gross.' I pointed to a shocking-pink headline on the mag. *'Five ways to send a boy to heaven with your kiss?'*

She snatched the mag away from me and slapped it on the pile. 'What do you want?'

'Peace on Earth and goodwill to all men.'

'Joel?!'

'All right. Dad said you wanted to see me.'

'Oh, yeah. That's right . . .' She took a moment to draw herself up, then crossing her arms in the manner of a girl who'd like to see me toasted on a fork, she said, 'I s'pose it was *you* who put him up to it, wasn't it?'

'What?'

'Joel, don't act it, OK?'

I flipped a hand. 'What are you talking about?'

She snatched a yellow notelet off her bedside table. A notelet with galloping horses on the front. 'This.'

'So?'

'It came while you were out.'

'*So?*' I repeated. What was it with girls? Why did they always expect you to guess what was in their devious girly minds?

Her scowl drilled into me. 'You *know* who it's from.'

Fine. OK. Mind-reading class. Nobody wound Maddie up like . . . 'Kenny?'

Her nostrils flared.

'Kenny wrote you a letter? He never told me.'

'Oh, sure. Oink. Oink. There flies a pig.'

'Seriously, he didn't. What does it say?'

With a petulant sniff, she flipped it open. '*Dear Madalene*— Oh, and he spelled it wrong. *I'm sorry to hear about your leg. I hope it gets better soon. I broke my little finger once. It's cool. I can make it crack in the rain.*' She tilted her head and glowered at me hard.

'He can,' I said. 'It's really freaky. Sounds like you're walking on cornflakes when he does it.'

'Joel, I don't want to know, OK?' She shuddered (for effect) and looped her hair. '*I wondered if I could come round and visit you? Joel says you get dead bored.'*

'Well, you do,' I said as she paused again. Since the big financial clampdown, her mobile had been sitting redundantly on her table, only taking incoming calls and texts. And she herself had kept visits from friends to a minimum; she didn't like to be seen in a helpless state.

'I could bring a game. Do you like Mousetrap?' She thumped the note down. 'This is a total wind-up, isn't it? The pair of you taking the mick, 'cos I'm hurt?'

I shook my head, but I couldn't help laughing. Kenny and Maddie playing Mousetrap? That would be one for the family album. 'He's just being friendly. You know how much he likes you.'

'He's a creep. He's stalking me. Tell him to get lost.' She scrunched the letter up and threw it at my chest. 'Tell the stupid geek I've got tons to do, *thank you.*' She pointed to a pile of note-books on the floor.

'That's homework,' I said. Her best mate, Fran, had been bringing it round, so she wouldn't fall too far behind with her lessons. 'You can't do school stuff all the time.'

'Well, I can hardly go out riding, can I? Or run? Or train to be a gymnast any more?' She ripped a tissue from a box and forced it to her nose. 'I *hate* this. Why can't I be normal again?' She jerked the bad leg, dislodging the sock.

On impulse, I helped it off. 'You will, soon. It's getting tons better.' In the early days, her foot had looked truly horrendous: a purple-yellow mass of ugly bruises that had made her physically sick when she saw them. Now the blood was slowly receding and her size six pinkies were looking less like jellybeans, more like human digits again. I reached out and wiggled her toes.

Her face froze with shocked disbelief. 'What are you doing?'

'Keeping your circulation going.'

She pulled her foot away. 'Only Mum does that.'

'Maddie, I'm your brother. It's OK. It's allowed. Anyway, Mum needs a rest sometimes.'

'What's that s'posed to mean?'

'She's stressed.'

'So am I!'

'Oh yeah, right! All you do is sit around reading books.' I glanced at her crutches, standing in the corner. 'You can walk now, can't you?'

'No, I can hobble. There's a difference. Trust me.'

Tch, she was such a pain sometimes. Resisting the urge to slap her one, I said, 'Why don't you come down and watch the telly one night? Mum and Dad would be really pleased.'

And something wild flashed across her eyes. Some demon lodging in the shadows of her mind got up and jumped from one pupil to the other. 'Huh, you mean we've still *got* a telly?'

Nice taunt, but I knew it was a cover. 'Are you OK?' I asked. 'You look a bit freaked.'

Out came her very best Year Nine gawp. 'Hel-lo? My *leg* is broken.'

Covering again. Something was spooking her. Something to do with getting up. 'You can make it to the bathroom and Erin's room. So why don't you come downstairs for a bit?'

'Because I like it up here, OK?'

'Staring out of the window?'

'What's wrong with that?'

I parted the curtains. 'Oh, there appears to be a leaf falling. Wow.'

'Funnee,' she said, crossing her arms tightly. 'You can see loads of stuff from up here, actually. There's this ginger-haired bloke who sits in his white van across the road, reading a paper for hours and hours.'

'Thrilling,' I said.

'I think he's a spy.'

'Yeah, right. And his name's Alex Rider and he works for MI6.'

Her mouth slid into a sneer. 'Tell you what else

I saw: my baby brother and his pretty little girl-friend.'

'You—'

'Ha. Now who's got the jits?' She laughed and waggled a victorious finger. 'Don't try to deny it. You walked her past the other night. She was still in her uniform. Very cute. Didn't have the guts to bring her in, though, did you?'

'I—'

'Mum wants to meet her. She said so after your little outburst. You've got to bring her round for tea. How sweet.'

'Fine,' I said, shrugging. 'I'm seeing her on Sunday. I'll bring her round then. Give you an excuse to get out of this pit.' I picked up her nightie case and flipped it at her. She caught it and hurled it back at my head.

'Oi!' I cried. I didn't think I deserved *that* amount of venom.

'I'm not coming down till I'm ready!' she snapped, and the demon was back in her eyes again. 'You can bring her up here. It's allowed. OK?'

I shook my head. 'See her at the table, like everyone else.'

She choked a tissue deep within her fist. 'I *can't*, stupid!' She bounced her cast.

Stupid? That was sisterly. 'Dad'll help you down.'

'No.'

'He will. Stop logging it, Maddie.'

'Get out,' she said suddenly.

'What?'

'Get out.'

'Why, what have I done?'

'Get out! Get out! GET OUT!'

I stumbled to the door and she started to weep. Erin came flying in, hearing the shouting. She saw Maddie in tears and dragged me away.

'What's going on? What's wrong with her?' I asked.

Erin shook her head and put a finger to her lips. When I was silent she pointed down the landing.

'What?' I hissed.

'Them,' she hissed back, walking her fingers in downward steps.

My heart missed a beat. Of course. The stairs.

Maddie was frightened of the stairs.

CHAPTER FIFTEEN

I asked Mum about it the next day at breakfast.

'I know,' she said, anxiously bunching a tea towel. 'I'm hoping it's just a temporary problem. Don't tease her about it. You'll only make things worse.'

I nodded and chewed on a triangle of toast. 'When does she have to go back to the hospital?'

'Soon. Hurry up. You don't want to miss your bus.'

I put the toast down. The birds could have it. 'She says you want to meet Roopindar.'

'If you're happy to bring her over, yes.' Her voice trailed into the fridge.

'Can she come for tea – on Sunday afternoon?'

'Sunday,' she muttered, glancing at the calendar. 'Erm, yes. That should be all right.'

'Can Kenny come too?'

'Kenny?'

'My *mate*?'

'Oh . . . yes,' she said again, 'of course he can.' She touched her temple as if her head was approaching overload status.

Poor Mum. Not quite here again. It never used to be like this. I felt her arm. 'Are you *sure* it's OK?'

She squeezed my hand. 'Sunday, five o'clock. Roopindar and Kenny. Chicken drumsticks. Kenny's favourite. Don't be late.'

Percy Arnold's house sat right on the peak of Clumber Hill. A little top hat on a fat potato, that was Kenny's assessment of it. To me and Roo it was a large old cottage with off-white walls and darkly latticed fairy-tale windows. I'd always been impressed by its deep thatched roof which looked, from a distance, like a frozen mudslide. The dry stone drive that led to the cottage boomeranged across a wide green field dotted with zillions of buttercups and daisies. For a millionaire's home, it was very unfussy.

'Are you sure this is it?' Roopindar asked.

I pointed to the leftmost dormer in the roof. A teddy bear was looking out from it.

We swung off our bikes and walked them up the drive. There was no gate to speak of, just a gap in the hedgerows that ran along the road. The horse chestnut tree we often stole the conkers from rustled its branches as we halted by the porch. Nervously, I clattered the large brass knocker.

The door swung open. Two cats, one ginger,

the other white and fluffy, poured out like the first streams of water through a lock gate.

'Oh,' went Roopindar, watching where they ran.

I kept my eyes fixed on Percy Arnold.

On the way here, we'd discussed what we thought an ice-cream millionaire ought to look like. Tall and handsome with manicured eyebrows – that was Roopindar's suggestion. Hair that spiralled upwards like soft whippy ice-cream – that was Kenny's idea.

Mr Arnold was nothing like either.

He was small, but stocky, with wispy strands of gingerish hair rising off his freckled scalp. Dressed in light grey trousers and a plain check shirt, he could have been anyone's ageing grandad, just woken up from a sleep in his chair. There were morsels of food in the corners of his mouth and ragged holes in the toes of his slippers. His face, as round as a bowling ball, would have been forgettable but for one thing: his bright blue swimmy eyes. They looked like small jewels, floating in jelly. I noticed straight away that he hardly ever blinked them. That spooked me a bit, especially when he turned them on me and said, 'You must be Joel.'

I said hello, nervously, and shook his hand.

Kenny took a pace forward. 'How did you know *I* wasn't Joel?'

Mr Arnold looked him steadily up and down. 'He has a rucksack on his back, in which I assume he's carrying the bear. Leave your bikes here. They'll be quite safe.'

We propped them underneath a window box packed full of fluttering violet flowers and trooped past him, single file, into the house. The hallway had a comforting woody smell and creaked underfoot like a fishing boat. Photographs of old-fashioned golfers filled the walls. There wasn't a hint of ice-cream anywhere.

'The room on the left,' Mr Arnold said.

Dup, dup, dup. My trainers thudded against the polished wooden floor. The sound echoed along a low, dipped ceiling, supported by beams full of woodworm holes. Red and gold paper lined the walls. Small spotlights picked out family portraits. It reminded me a bit of a stately home. Opposite the door was an empty fireplace, big enough for even the fattest Santa. And in one corner was a throne-like chair, with pale green padding and quilted cushions. Kenny was about to park himself in it when Mr Arnold caught him by the arm and said, 'No, I'd prefer it if you sat over here.' He guided Kenny to the sofa by the window. Roopindar sat next to him, smoothing her jeans. I plonked myself down in the armchair beside them, with my rucksack on the floor, wedged tight between my knees. Stretched out on the floral cushions behind me was yet another cat.

Mr Arnold crossed the room to a large old sideboard where some tea things and a range of fancy cakes had been set out on a silver tray. 'I haven't prepared for three,' he said, in an elegant voice with a slight Welsh accent, 'so cakes will have to be rationed, I'm afraid.'

We all started to burble at once, telling him politely it didn't matter.

'No, no. I insist,' he said, in a tone which suggested he'd planned this to perfection and would have his own way, whatever we said. He opened a cupboard in search of more crockery. 'Joel, why don't you introduce your friends?'

'This is Roopindar,' I said, sitting forward. I pointed to her, even though he wasn't looking.

'She's his girlfriend,' said Kenny. 'I'm his best mate.'

'And this is Kenny,' I said, as if Kenny ever needed any kind of introduction.

'Good,' said Mr Arnold, polishing a teacup on the sleeve of his shirt. 'Joel, Roopindar and Kenny. Good.' He put the tray onto a trolley and wheeled it over. 'And do you all share an interest in bears?'

'Not exactly,' said Roo. 'Me and Kenny are here because—'

'We want to see how much it's worth,' Kenny blurted.

Mr Arnold smiled thinly, just enough to conceal his obvious disappointment. 'Yes, of course. It must be quite exciting for you, to be in possession of something so special.' He clicked a pair of serving tongs at Roo.

She studied the cakes. There were six to choose from, six edible gift boxes, coated in different shades of marzipan. 'The green one,' she whispered.

'Good choice,' he assured her, making her blush. He went to Kenny next. Then to me. I had a white one with a cherry on top.

For a while we ate cake and drank millionaire's tea. Mr Arnold stood by the fireplace throughout, resting his elbow on the mantelpiece above it. He chatted freely and was even persuaded to talk about ice-cream, how he'd loved it as a boy and how making it was all he'd ever wanted to do. 'I expect you'd like to know if it's true,' he said. He gave us all an enquiring look, then settled on Kenny as if he knew that Kenny was the one most likely to pop the question.

Kenny gave out a dumb-sounding, 'What?'

'Whether I mix it with my foot or not?'

For once, Kenny was left completely speechless.

Mr Arnold drew up his trouser leg. 'It's false,' he said. 'Lost the real thing in a car accident. Haven't made a single ice-cream since; all done now by my eldest son. So the rumour is as phoney as the leg, I'm afraid. Couldn't let you go without knowing that, could I?'

'No,' said Kenny, sounding genuinely grateful. 'What about your other foot?'

'Kenny!' Roopindar knocked his knee.

Mr Arnold changed the subject. 'So, according to my friend Laurence Lucan, you have a twenties Horace bear to show me.'

'Yes,' I said, spilling cake crumbs on the carpet. Another cat appeared and started licking them up. Its tail kept flicking under my chin as I undid the rucksack and lifted the flap.

At the sight of the famous big round ears, Mr Arnold took an equally big round breath. 'Yes, that's certainly a Horace,' he said. 'It looks a little ragged. May I ask how you came by it?'

'It's ... my grandma's,' I said.

Mr Arnold nodded and sipped his tea. His eyes looked for mine above the rim of his cup. 'Since childhood?'

'Erm. I think so. Yes.'

'Then she must be quite elderly? Well into her seventies?'

I glanced at Kenny. 'She's dead,' he said.

'Oh, I'm so sorry,' Mr Arnold replied.

Not half as sorry as me. Both my grans were still *alive*. I glared at Kenny and he shrugged as if to say, 'Well, the oldie doesn't know.' Maybe not, but it didn't stop me feeling that I'd got the word 'fraud' stamped in red capitals across my forehead. I drew Horace out and bumped him on my lap. 'This is him.'

Mr Arnold finished his tea and placed his cup and saucer on the fire surround. Slipping his hands into his trouser pockets, he turned and set his gaze fully on Horace. For a second or two, all seemed well. I watched him admiring Horace's shape, starting at the legendary over-sized ears and passing down his body to the threadbare foot pads. But then he blinked. And blinked again. And suddenly his eyes frosted over like ice. It was just as if his brain had crashed to a halt and his thoughts were as solid as his artificial leg. We all waited for the expert on bears to speak, but though his pale lips parted, they formed no words.

'Do you want to have a closer look?'

I offered Horace up but Mr Arnold turned away, twisting a gold ring on his finger. 'He's damaged,' he muttered. 'How did that happen?'

'His gran had a pit bull terrier,' said Kenny.

Miaow went the cat behind me and leaped off the chair. Even Roo sat up with a start and had to grab at her plate to save it sliding off her lap.

I spiked Kenny's eyes with the fiercest look I knew. 'What?' he gestured. *What?* I ask you. A pit bull had savaged Horace? What a thing to say to a man who loved bears. 'The dog didn't chew his arm,' I said.

'He's just been loved a lot,' said Roo, doing her best to come to my rescue.

'My sister, Erin, she cuddles him,' I added, 'but I'm going to save up and get him mended.'

Mr Arnold touched a hand to the bridge of his nose. 'So you can make more profit when you sell him?'

'No,' I said, getting more and more anxious. I could feel Mr Arnold's growing resentment like a sudden, bitter change in the weather. 'I love him. Honestly. I want to keep him. It's just . . .'

Then Kenny lunged in and finished it dead. 'Mr Lucan said *you* might want to buy him. We could sell him a bit cheaper, 'cos he needs cleaning.'

And that seemed to hit Mr Arnold the hardest. He wheeled away sharply with a fist to his mouth. 'No, I won't be buying him, thank you.'

For a moment, the only sound in the room was the lazy tick of a grandfather clock. Mr Arnold stood quite still, as if he couldn't make sense of anything we'd said. On the wall in front of him was a photographic portrait of an elderly lady with thick blonde hair. I guessed it was his wife, but I didn't dare ask. As I watched him lift his gaze towards it, a peculiar ripple of fear passed through me; the sort of wrenching panic you feel when you *know* something's wrong but you can't quite place it. I rubbed Horace's ear and wished I'd never brought him. Mr Arnold extended a hand.

'I will have a look at him now, if I may?' His voice was curt. Not asking. Commanding. He took Horace from me and examined his label by the light from the window. Then, with a delicate press of his finger, he pushed the loose eye back into its socket. He took Horace over to the chair in the corner and sat him beside a plain green cushion. 'He was Grandma's bear, you say?'

I looked at Kenny. A glance that said 'shut it'. 'Yes.'

'Did she ever talk to you about his eyes?'

'Eyes?' whispered Roo, looking a bit uncomfortable.

Mr Arnold's hard unflinching stare panned like a searchlight across our faces.

I shuddered and shook my head.

'Well, I'm surprised about that,' he said, as if it was no surprise at all. 'I take it Mr Lucan explained to you that all the first batches of Horace bears were made with modest changes of detail?'

I nodded slowly.

'Good,' he replied, letting the word slip out through his teeth. 'This a series seven bear. It's their stare that makes them so collectable.' He stepped sideways so we could all view Horace on his throne. 'They're really quite famous for it. It used to be said that if you looked into this stare from exactly the right slant, the bear would peer into the depths of your soul and invite you to confess all your wickedness and sins.'

'That's spooky,' said Kenny, picking his nose.

'Quite,' said Mr Arnold. 'Perhaps you'd like to try?'

'No way,' Kenny snorted, reeling back. A white cat hissed at him over its shoulder. Mr Arnold bent down and picked it up.

'It was the size of the pupils that did it,' he said, stroking the cat like the James Bond villain, 'and the distance the eyes were set apart on the face. It gave the whole series a unique appearance that other manufacturers often tried to copy but none were ever able to reproduce. People said there was something . . . unearthly about it. You must have heard the fairy tale? One of you? Surely?'

The white cat started to purr.

All of us shook our heads.

'It was rumoured,' Mr Arnold said darkly, 'that William Horace tore his own eyes out of their sockets and used those initially instead of the glass ones, leaving them in place for one night only so that each of the bears could inherit his piety.'

'His what?' asked Kenny.

'Godliness,' Roopindar explained, looking sick.

Mr Arnold tilted his head. 'How about it, Joel? Are you in the mood for baring your soul? What do you see when you look into these eyes?'

'He looks homesick,' I muttered without stopping to think.

For the second time in minutes Mr Arnold froze. There was pain behind his eyes, but I didn't know why. So I turned my gaze completely on Horace. Eyes set, he did look curiously holy. I thought back quickly to how I'd found him. Everything we'd been involved in together seemed to go tumbling through my mind, as though I was twisting a kaleidoscope of memories. But right at its centre was an ugly black hole. Inside the hole lay the seeds of my dishonesty, the wickedness and sin Mr Arnold was talking about. Something wasn't right here. I knew it instinctively. The old man didn't believe my story. But why should it really matter to him? My head was still wrangling with the threads of that question when a puffy grey cat leaped onto the chair, stumbling over Horace's outstretched legs. The eye popped forward on his cheek again. Instantly, the spell was broken.

Mr Arnold knew it, too. He put the white cat down and moved Horace to my lap. 'He was made in nineteen twenty-one,' he said. 'He was a luxury purchase and his price would have been approximately eight shillings and eleven pence. I shouldn't think that means very much to you. What price did Mr Lucan put on his head?'

'Eight thousand pounds.'

The blue eyes wandered into the distance. 'Then he's a little off the mark. This bear, properly restored, would be worth nearly four times that amount.'

'Thirty thousand?' Roopindar gasped.

Percy Arnold smiled like a well-oiled machine. 'Yes. I expect Joel's grandma will be very pleased to hear about that . . .'

CHAPTER SIXTEEN

'That guy was seriously weird,' said Kenny as the three of us jumped off our bikes at home.

'Not weird,' said Roopindar, unbuckling her hat, 'just . . . I don't know, troubled somehow.'

I propped my bike against Kenny's and said, 'I don't think it helped when you asked if he'd like to buy Horace off us.'

Roo gave a sharp whistle. 'Yeah! Did you see his face when you said that? He looked dead hurt. *And* when Joel said Horace looked homesick. Why do you think that was?'

'Who cares?' said Kenny, opening the door that led through to the garden.

'Hi,' said a disembodied voice. Erin was stumping up the lawn, balancing on a pair of stilts.

'Wow,' laughed Roo. 'Joel didn't tell me his sisters were so tall.'

Erin smiled and did a little dance. 'Do you want a go?'

'No, thanks.'

'Kenny will,' I said, shoving him forward.

'Get lost,' he grumbled.

'I'll teach you,' begged Erin, jumping down.

'Erin, leave him be,' said Mum, appearing on the back step, sweeping some bread crumbs off a plate, 'we don't want any more broken bones.'

'Yeah, how's Maddie?' Kenny asked brightly, stepping deliberately in front of Erin. She poked him in the back until he moved aside.

'Maddie is upstairs, resting,' said Mum. 'You can see her later. No sneaking in on your way to the bathroom. Hello, Roopindar. Welcome to the madhouse. Come and sit inside. It's looking like rain.'

Into the kitchen we went. Even though tea was half an hour away, we arranged ourselves around the table to wait. Mum and Roo were chattering like long-lost friends, and Erin was trashing Kenny at Scissors, Paper, Stone, when Dad walked in with a cheery greeting. He shook Roo's hand and exchanged a few words, then immediately switched the talk to Horace.

'So, how did your meeting go?' He plucked a grape from a bunch by the fridge, tossed it in the air and caught it in his mouth. 'What did Mr Arnold have to say?'

Kenny looked up. There was absolute silence, apart from the sound of Mum chopping veg.

'Come on, don't keep us in suspense,' said

Dad. 'If you want it insured, I'll need to know its value.'

'Are you talking about Horace?' Erin turned her head and looked accusingly at me. 'Where have you been with him?'

Dad draped his arms loosely around her neck and gathered her into the slope of his body. 'They've been to see a millionaire who knows about bears.'

'You'd better not have sold him!' Erin cried out.

'Erin, turn the volume down,' said Mum.

'We haven't sold him,' Roo said kindly.

To prove it, I took Horace out of my rucksack and sat him on the table with his back to the wall.

Dad pressed on: 'So, how much is Winnie here worth? And tell me truthfully, because if I cover it for a false amount you won't get a penny if anyone steals him or the house burns down.'

I looked across at Kenny and saw him tense. I really was on the spot this time. This time there could be no untruths. 'Thirty thousand,' I said.

Mum's knife stopped hitting the chopping board.

'Pounds?' Erin queried, screwing up her nose.

I gulped at Dad.

His face was expressionless, but not his voice. 'Don't play games with me, Joel.'

'It's true,' said Kenny. 'He's dead old and rare. You'd have to clean him up to get the full amount, though.'

'Oh my God,' Mum panted, clutching at the worktop. Her face had turned the colour of the mushrooms she was slicing.

'Are you OK? Do you want some help?' asked Roo.

Dad answered for her. 'Thank you, Roopindar, Mrs Hadleigh will be fine. Why don't you lot disappear for a while?' He slid his hands along Erin's arms and let go of her as if he'd sent a bird into flight. 'Joel, take Roopindar up to see Maddie.'

'I'll take her,' offered Kenny, springing to his feet.

'No, you won't,' Erin grumbled, holding him back. She took Roo's arm and led her down the hall, Kenny clipping their heels in pursuit.

'Joel?' Dad called me back as I stood up to follow.

I paused at the door.

'What exactly are you planning to do with this bear?'

I glanced at Horace, sitting upright on the table. 'I plan to draw him,' I said.

*   *   *

It wasn't the answer Dad was expecting, but it was smart enough to buy some space between us. I sank into the shadows and hurried upstairs, just in time to see a cushion flying out of Maddie's room.

Kenny caught it against his chest. 'I can't get out! I'm already on the landing!'

Another cushion bounced off the upright of the door.

'Stay out here,' I advised him as I pushed my way in.

Erin was busily explaining to Roo that Maddie and Kenny didn't get on.

'We do,' said Kenny.

'We so do not,' Maddie said with a hiss, her face as fixed as an old ship's figurehead. She turned her dark-eyed frown on me. 'I cannot believe you've let him see my room!'

'Can I look at your books?' Kenny's plaintive voice drifted in from the landing.

'Erin, shut the door,' said Maddie.

'Why? He's not dangerous.'

Maddie gave her a look.

Roopindar waved her hands for calm. 'Erm, hi. My name's Roo. I'm new around here.'

'Hi,' Maddie grunted. 'Like your thumb ring.'

'Thanks. Mind if I perch for a bit?'

Maddie hotched to one side of the bed, still sending fireballs out through the doorway.

'Lads, they're such a pain,' she carped.

'Oh, forget about them,' said Roo. 'How's your leg?'

Maddie shrugged and they started to talk about the accident. It was odd, hearing her describe what had happened, reliving the horror of that awful day. She'd never discussed it in depth with me, and I felt like a stranger as she opened up to Roo. But I sensed it was doing her some good to let it out, so I didn't butt in, and neither did Erin, except to fill in a little detail here and there.

Within a few minutes, all three girls were so engrossed that none of them saw Kenny edge his way in. On tip-toe, like lunch in the lion's den, he moved around taking stock of my sister's life: her wall-to-wall posters of heavy-metal bands, her make-up, her shoes, her mini-disc collection, the three porcelain dolls which occupied a cube of her built-in shelving, her array of scented candles, her *Stargirl* T-shirt (he grinned at that). It was touching to see him drinking her in. For the first time ever, I realized how much he really liked her and how brave he must be to keep bouncing her insults. I mouthed him to be careful as he brushed against her jewellery tree and nearly felled it. He backed away to study her collection of books, and was innocently poring over the spines when she saw him and barked, 'Erm, what are you doing?'

'You like Paddington,' he said.

Maddie turned her head to one side. 'I don't believe this. So?'

'*I* like Paddington. That means we've got something in common.'

'Kenny reads to his little sister,' I said.

'Do you?' asked Erin, sitting up like a meerkat.

'Him? Read?' Maddie crossed her arms and sneered.

And that was her big mistake. As it happened, Kenny was an excellent reader. He was always being chosen to read passages from the Bible in school assemblies. Blushing, he rose to the challenge. 'This is the best of the series, I think.' He slipped a copy of *Paddington at Large* off the shelf. 'I like the story where Paddington's on a game show with this bloke called Ronnie Playfair; Jess likes it when I do his voice.'

'You do voices?' laughed Roo, looking slightly astonished.

Kenny gave an awkward shrug. His red cheeks simmered to another shade of crimson. 'It makes the story more fun, that's all.'

'Show us,' begged Erin.

'Yeah, do,' Roo chorused.

Maddie feigned nausea and covered her face.

But none of that was going to stop Kenny now. He found the story he'd been talking about, sat down next to Erin and read to us as if we were six years old. It was brilliant, like listening to someone off the telly. Roo and Erin giggled with delight as his voice kept changing between the characters: deep and pompous for Ronnie Playfair; innocent and slightly cute for Paddington. He performed two hilarious pages and stopped.

'No, go on,' worshipped Erin, bunching her hands underneath her chin.

Roo applauded loudly and turned to Maddie. 'Good, isn't he?'

My sister pushed out her bottom lip. 'He could have picked a better book,' she moaned. '*Paddington Goes to Town* is easily the best.'

Kenny tugged it off the shelf. 'Shall I read from that, then?'

Maddie's brown eyes flickered uncertainly. I was stunned. She was actually *thinking* about it.

Annoyingly, the moment was broken by Dad. 'Joel? Where are you?' His voice ranged up from the bottom of the stairs.

'Which story?' asked Kenny, flipping through the book.

'I haven't said you can yet,' Maddie hit back.

But neither had she said he couldn't. Weird.

*   *   *

136

Dad was in the hall with his arms loosely folded, pressing one foot against the bottom stair. 'You got a minute, Joel?'

It was a command, not a question. But I stood my ground. 'Why? What for?'

'I want to talk to you – in the front room.'

'Oh, Dad! Roopindar's here. Can't we do it after tea?'

'Tell Roopindar it won't take long.'

I dragged myself back to Maddie's room, muttering.

Roo met me at the door. 'Hey, what's up?'

'Dad: he wants to see me.'

'Why?'

'Dunno. Have those two driven you barmy yet?' In the room, Maddie and Kenny were arguing loudly about Mr Curry, Paddington's neighbour.

Roo grinned and said, 'Nah, it's good fun. Maddie's cool. Dead savvy. Want to know something major?'

'Yeah, like what?'

'Like Maddie really likes Kenny, that's what.'

'*What?! No way!*'

'Sssh!' she hissed, and pulled the door to. 'Honest. No dissing. You can tell by the way she watches him while he's reading. She might look bored, but her eyes are all . . . dizzy with admiration. She's only acting grumpy because it wouldn't be cool to admit she fancies someone in the year below hers.'

'You're mental. Maddie wouldn't go out with *Kenny*.'

She flapped me again to keep my voice down. 'Course she wouldn't; her mates would scorch her. Doesn't stop her having a thing for him, though.'

'Maddie and Kenny?'

'Solid. Trust me. Takes a girl to know.'

'Joel, come on.' Dad's voice rose from the hall once more.

'No way,' I said, and backed away, laughing. Maddie and Kenny?

Solid, mouthed Roo.

Dad took me into the front room and closed the door. Mum was on the edge of the sofa, looking tense. On the coffee table, staring into space, sat Horace.

'Sit down,' Dad said.

I chose the seat next to Mum. She patted my knee.

Dad stood by the fireplace, rubbing the muscles at the back of his neck. 'I want to talk to you about this bear.'

Not again. I made my sigh a little too obvious and Dad said, 'This is important, Joel. If Mr Arnold is correct, then Horace is the single most valuable item in this house. That means he's going to be costly to insure. As you know, we're trying to cut back at the moment.'

So that was it. The money thing again. 'It's not my fault he's worth so much.'

'No, I realize that,' he said. 'Nevertheless, it's an issue we need to address . . . if you were planning on keeping him, that is.'

My spine straightened up like a nail. 'I'm not selling him, Dad. He's mine. I want him.'

'Exactly,' said Mum. 'Trevor, this is wrong.'

Dad overruled her with a sweep of his hand. 'Joel, listen to me carefully now. When you bought this bear, fifty pence is as much as you thought he was worth. He was a project for art and nothing more. How long would it have been before the novelty wore off and he was on his way back to a charity shop, anyway?'

'I *like* him.'

'Yes, we've established that. But think about all the other things you like. Things we could lose if our circumstances don't change.'

'Trevor, this isn't fair,' Mum said. 'You can't use emotional blackmail on your son.'

'I'm not,' said Dad, clearly disappointed that she wasn't on his side. 'I'm trying to make him see that we have an opportunity here to put the family back on track.'

'Then why did you stop me selling my thimbles?'

'That would have raised just a few hundred pounds.'

'So? The principle's the same. You wouldn't let me give up my most treasured possession, even though I wanted to do it for the family. We'll find a way round it, you said. What's the difference with Horace and Joel?'

'The difference,' he said, reddening round the collar, 'is the shortfall in our mortgage. The difference is a happy, stress-free home.' He turned to me again. 'I'm sorry, Joel. I don't care how attached you are to Horace, you're not old enough or responsible enough to make a decision about something worth that amount of money.'

'What do you mean?'

'I mean—' He paused as the doorbell rang. Feet pounded down the stairs. Erin: doorbell fairy, doing her job. 'I mean, I'm going to make the decision for you. In a few months' time, if the financial outlook hasn't improved, I'm going to have to ask you to sell the bear. And if you won't . . . for the good of us all, *I* will.'

'No!' I shouted, jumping to my feet. I snatched at Horace and his loose arm came away. 'I'll bury this! Where no one can find it. Then he won't be worth *anything* and you'll be really—'

'Dad?' Erin's face appeared at the door. She was shaking and her skin was as white as milk.

'What's the matter?' asked Mum, looking up, looking anxious. 'Erin, what's wrong?'

'The police are here,' she gulped. 'They're asking for Joel.'

CHAPTER SEVENTEEN

There were two of them. A burly man and a young blonde woman. Their uniforms crackled as they walked into the room. Mum made me stand aside to let them have the sofa. It was built for three people. Between them, they filled it.

'Thank you,' said the man. He took off his cap, revealing a head of short, black hair. He had hard grey eyes and a level jaw and looked as if he knew how to handle himself. On his belt were a pair of shining handcuffs. He unclipped his baton and laid it on the floor. 'I'm PC Taggart. This is WPC Janesmith. Are you Joel Hadleigh?'

'Yes, this is Joel, our son,' Dad answered. 'What's this about?'

'We're here about the theft of a bear,' said Janesmith, her manner blunt, her face expressionless. 'Cuddly, not grizzly.' Horace was still on the table in front of her; she hadn't even looked at him.

'Theft?' Mum put a hand to her mouth and

exchanged a fearful glance with Dad.

By now, Kenny and Roopindar had come downstairs and were in the hall, just outside the door. I couldn't help but flash a look their way. The policewoman saw it, saw them hovering, and with one stern finger beckoned them in. Erin hung back, biting a knuckle. Upstairs, Maddie shouted, 'Erin, what's happening?'

Dad gritted his teeth. 'Joel, start talking.'

'I didn't mean it,' I blurted. 'They were going to throw him out! I asked how much for him and they said fifty pence. So I put it in their tin. I didn't think anyone would mind if you took things out of a filthy old skip.'

'*Skip?* What skip? What are you talking about?'

I gulped at the policeman. His radio buzzed. He turned his cap silently through his hands.

'The one at the back of the charity shop. He was going to the tip. He was, Dad, honest.'

Dad looked at Horace, then at Kenny, then at me. 'You mean you stole it? The bear's not legally yours?'

'Oh, Joel,' sighed Mum.

Erin shot upstairs to Maddie.

'But they were chucking it,' said Kenny. 'That's not thieving, is it?'

Taggart sniffed and flexed the toes of his

giant black boots. 'The contents of a waste skip are the property of whoever hires it, son. It certainly qualifies as theft.' He let his tongue do a tour of his lips, then rolled his harsh gaze back towards me. There was something faintly smug about him now, as if I'd blabbed much more than he'd first anticipated. 'That's how you came by your bear then, is it? Lifted it out of a skip?'

'Well, don't you know?' Dad asked. 'Isn't that why you're here?'

The two officers exchanged a glance.

'This *is* the bear you're looking for, isn't it?' asked Dad. He aimed two fingers at Horace's ears.

Janesmith pulled a photograph out of her pocket. 'This is the bear we're looking for, Mr Hadleigh.' She laid the photo on the table next to Horace's paws.

And I thought for one horrible gut-wrenching moment that there was going to be another bear in the picture, and that I'd gone and confessed about Horace for nothing. But it was Horace all right, from another time: his fur as clean as freshly washed sand, his eyes set straight and sparkling with pride, ears neatly brushed, label unsoiled, arms and legs fixed properly in place, sitting in . . .

'Oh my God,' wailed Roopindar, catching

sight of the snap. She put her fists to her mouth in shock.

Mum hurried across to hold her. 'Roopindar, what's the matter?'

'He knew,' she quivered. 'He knew all the time.'

'Who did? What are you talking about?'

Meanwhile, Kenny was studying the picture. 'Hey, that looks like . . .'

'Mr Arnold's chair,' I breathed. The 'throne' Horace had sat in just an hour before. My heart began to thump against my ribs.

'Percy Arnold?' muttered Dad. 'What's he got to do with it?'

PC Janesmith opened a notebook. 'I have details here of the serial number on the label of the bear in the photograph. I think you'll find it matches the label on him.' She nodded straight-faced at Horace. 'Earlier this afternoon your son and his friends took an old teddy bear to Mr Arnold's house, asking him if he would value it for them. Mr Arnold recognized the bear at once and called us as soon as the children had gone.'

Dad stabbed a finger at Horace again. 'Are you saying this thing belongs to him?'

PC Taggart lifted an eyebrow.

Dad groaned and turned his face to the wall, dragging a hand from his forehead to his mouth. 'I don't believe I'm hearing this.' He swept a bitter look towards me and Kenny. 'You took the bear to be valued by the man who *owns* it?'

'We didn't know!' Kenny protested.

But that wasn't good enough for Dad. He launched into a rant that was as bad as anything I'd ever heard. It wasn't until Taggart knocked a knuckle on the table that the room fell silent and Janesmith was able to fill in the details.

'Two years ago,' she said, stretching her feet, 'Mr Arnold suffered a break-in at his home on Clumber Hill. Several items of antique jewellery were removed – plus a valuable collectors' bear. Nothing of the robbery was traced. Until now.'

'We didn't do it,' Kenny blurted out. 'We didn't nick the bear from *him*.'

'It's in your possession,' Taggart said coldly.

'Oh, come on,' Dad snorted, throwing up his hands. 'What exactly are you accusing them of?'

Taggart looked him straight in the eye. 'Try handling stolen goods – for a start.'

'That's ridiculous! They're just a bunch of kids!'

'Above the age of ten they can be charged, Mr Hadleigh.'

'Oh, God,' sobbed Roopindar. 'My dad's gonna kill me.'

Mum held her tight and lashed at the police. 'Even if what you're saying is true, they clearly didn't know that Horace was already stolen property. It's ludicrous to think they were involved in any break-in. Joel told you, he took the bear from a skip. It's only been in this house a matter of weeks. My son is not a liar.'

'Oh, really?' Janesmith threw Mum a vacant look. 'How's your mother, Mrs Hadleigh?'

'My mother?' Mum looked totally confused by the question.

'And yours, Mr Hadleigh? Is she with us or not?'

Dad screwed up his face. 'What are you talking about? Both our mothers are fit and well, thank you.'

'That's not what your son thinks,' Janesmith said.

Dad looked at me hard. I started to quake.

Janesmith continued, 'According to Mr Arnold's information, your son inherited the bear on his granny's deathbed – which side of the family, he didn't make clear. As for this one,' she pointed at Kenny, 'he tried to sell it to Mr Arnold at a knockdown price. Why should we believe a word they say?'

'You can check with the charity shop,' said

a voice. Erin was back in the doorway again, chewing her hair, half-hidden by the frame. 'They'll remember having Horace and that will prove that Joel and Kenny didn't steal him from Mr Arnold.'

PC Taggart cracked his knuckles. 'Just what we need: a mini Miss Marple. And who are you?'

'Our daughter,' Dad reacted crossly. 'She's got nothing to do with this, unless you count the fact that she's cuddled the bear a couple of times. Are you going to read her her rights, too?'

Janesmith took a pen from her jacket pocket and clicked it as if she'd set a time bomb ticking. 'We just want to get all the facts, Mr Hadleigh. This bear was the subject of an aggravated burglary. It was *Mrs* Arnold's most treasured possession. She was clinically traumatized by its loss. Four days after the robbery, she suffered a stroke from which she never recovered.'

'Oh, no,' breathed Mum.

Dad closed his eyes.

'Now, we'll need to hear statements from all three "kids". Then we'll decide what action, if any, needs to be taken.'

'What's going to happen to Horace?' asked Erin, a bright tear streaking down her cheek.

The policewoman looked him idly up and

down. 'Looks like he wants a bit of surgery to me.'

I was still holding the severed arm. Leaning forward, I rested it on Horace's legs.

'He's evidence; he'll go to forensics,' said Taggart. 'Find me a plastic bag, Mrs Hadleigh.'

CHAPTER EIGHTEEN

They were there for another two hours. While Kenny, Roo and Erin ate their over-cooked tea, and Maddie was brought up to speed on proceedings, the police wrote down all the details of my story. It covered three lined pages. They made me sign each sheet to say it was true, but refused to say whether they believed me or not, until they'd had a chance to talk to Doris in the shop. Most of their questions weren't about the shop. They asked me lots of times in several different ways what I'd intended to do with Horace. When I told them my plan had been to find his real owner, the man, PC Taggart, half-sneered and said, 'Well, you managed that, all right.' And that hurt. About Mr Arnold tricking us. Why couldn't he have said that Horace was his? Why couldn't he have just been overjoyed to see him and told us the truth instead of dumping us in it? Why did he have to go and rat on us like that?

For the next four days our house was like a dungeon while we waited and waited to hear my fate. Then, on a rainy Thursday night, PC Taggart returned without warning. He took me and my parents into the kitchen and spoke to them grimly as if I wasn't there, using terrifying expressions like 'young offenders' register' and 'Crown Prosecution Service'. But at the end of it he said no action would be taken. The charity shop had confirmed my story. And though I could technically be charged with petty theft, due to the extraordinary circumstances of the case, neither the police nor the charity were willing to pursue it – and all I'd get was a slapped wrist, anyway. Mum cried into a tea towel. I thought she'd never stop. While Dad tried to calm her, he asked about the other accusation, the one about us handling stolen goods. PC Taggart had picked up his cap, looked at us severely on his way to the door and said: 'Just be grateful you didn't try to sell the bear, otherwise you would have been in serious bother.' And then Dad was on the verge of crying, too. And I was never quite sure what had hit him the hardest: the know-ledge that one of us might have gone to jail or the misery of knowing that he'd suddenly lost the means to pay off all his debts.

'Well, it was a near miss, for sure,' said Mr Reynolds, back from his illness, back acting as my 'counsellor' again at school. 'All of this could have been avoided, you know, if you hadn't gone and spun me that line about your gran. If you'd been honest and told me you'd pinched him, I would have advised you to take the bear back to that skip straight away, no question.'

'I know,' I said, and lowered my head.

He pushed a small bundle of brushes towards me and asked me to wash them out at the sink. 'What's the fall-out like at home?'

'Bad,' I said, running the tap. 'Dad's dead gloomy; he hardly ever talks. Mum's trying hard, but she cries a lot and just keeps wanting to sleep all the time; she's going to the doctor's this morning. Erin cooked tea for me and Maddie last night.'

Mr Reynolds raised both eyebrows together. 'Well, one good housepoint for Erin, then. How *is* Maddie now?'

'Her leg doesn't hurt, but she's frightened of the stairs. She hasn't been down since the day she came home.'

'She's going to have to, to have her cast off,' he said.

I nodded. 'I know.' Everyone knew. It was the latest source of anxiety in the house: what was going to happen when Maddie's hospital appointment came round?

Mr Reynolds let it pass. 'And what about you? How's it going with Roopindar?'

How did *he* know about Roopindar? My cheeks turned as red as the paint running out of the hairs of the brushes.

Smiling, he confided: 'You're the talk of the staff room, Joel. Romantic liaisons never go unnoticed.'

They would now. 'I'm not allowed to talk to her, sir.'

'Ah,' he said, clamping his teeth as if he could have been a little more sensitive. 'I suppose her parents think her involvement with Horace has brought some level of shame upon the family?'

Too right. I would never forget her father's look when he'd called at the house to pick her up. The harshness of his stare could have frightened off a vampire. If he'd come with his *kirpan* tucked inside his belt I would still be running now, fearing a scalping. She had rung him to say what had happened, of course, dotting her Punjabi with frantic words of English. From her expression alone I could tell she was going to be in trouble at home. Given the choice, she might have opted for a cell in the police station that night. After the call, Mum had crouched down and asked her quietly, 'Will you be all right?' Roo had emptied her tear ducts all over Mum's top, crying out about the terrible disgrace to her family and how she'd never be allowed to see me again. Mum reached for my hand and made me stroke Roo's hair. It was the closest I'd ever been to her. I didn't stop stroking till the doorbell rang and her father swept in. He exchanged brief words with my parents and the cops, then walked her away with his hands on her shoulders. When she tried to look back, he pointed her ahead. I knew there and then our relationship was finished.

'Such a lot of needless suffering,' Mr Reynolds sighed, 'all for the sake of a blooming teddy. You know what I'd like to know? The one question no one's been able to answer: how did he get into the charity shop in the first place?'

I dried all the brushes and left them on the rack. 'The police asked Doris that. All she can remember is that Horace was dumped outside in a bag, with some old clothes and jigsaws and stuff.'

Mr Reynolds did his favourite detective trick of pulling the end of his nose into a point. 'So our robber didn't know what the bear was worth, either? No self-respecting thief is going to give thirty grand of swag away to charity, are they?'

Before I could comment, Kenny bowled in, taking a disgustingly large bite from a bright red apple.

'And talking of swag,' Mr Reynolds said dryly. 'Kenneth Edgar Jones. Notorious, of this parish. Have you come to see me or your partner in crime?'

'Joel,' he said, and yanked me out into the corridor. He fished in his pocket. 'You've gotta look at this.'

It was a postcard picturing Paddington Bear. 'Kenny,' I tutted, 'you've gotta stop sending Maddie letters.'

He grinned like a whale. 'Didn't. Turn it over.'

On the back were a few neat lines of writing . . . Maddie's writing.

Dear Kenny,

I know it's taken ages but I haven't felt like doing much since I broke my leg. I just wanted to say thanks for your get well card and for reading to me from Paddington last week. You were good. It cheered me up. But Mr Curry is not a cool character. You are totally random sometimes. You do his voice well, though. See you soon, Maddie x

'Wow,' I gasped. 'She wrote to you.'

'Look at that,' he chirped, and pointed to the small *x* after her name.

'Kenny, don't get your hopes up, OK? She always signs her name with a soppy little kiss.'

'Don't care,' he beamed, nicking the card back from me and fixing his pouting lips to the ink.

E-yoo. I punched his shoulder. Hard.

'Let me come round tonight,' he begged. 'You can't say she doesn't want to see me now, can you?'

'It's a thank-you note, not a love letter, you twonk!' I walked away, rattling the fins of a radiator. 'Anyway, you can't come round tonight; I've got art club. And Dad'll be working. And Mum's going to Erin's school concert.'

'So Maddie's on her own, you mean?'

'She's a big girl, Kenny. She can cope for an hour.'

'Yeah, s'pose,' he said, and crunched into his apple.

And I should have known then that his perky little shrug was not to be trusted. As the day rolled on, he didn't mention Maddie or the post-card again. Not at lunchtime, lying flat out on the playing fields. Not in chemistry, while we gazed in boredom at a crystal of copper sulphate, waiting for it to 'grow'. And at the end of school, instead of pestering me to death about when he could come for tea the next time, he merely hitched up his bag, stuck his thumb out and said, 'See ya,' before disappearing into the fast lane of blazers.

For my part, I didn't think any more about it – until I arrived home, first, that night and found the kitchen door ajar. In itself, there was nothing unusual in that. It was the crunch of glass underfoot that chilled me, and the jagged hole in the lower left pane, the one through which a hand had reached and turned the brass door key upside down . . .

CHAPTER NINETEEN

Voices. I could hear muffled voices upstairs. The intruder must be talking to Maddie. What was he saying? Was he threatening my sister? Attacking her, perhaps? She must be scared to death. My head pounded. My body rocked with fear. What should I do? The police. I had to call the police. Phone. In the front room. 999. But what if he heard me? What to do then? My cricket bat. It was standing in the corner of the kitchen. I picked it up quietly. If I had to, I'd hit.

On tip-toes, I made it into the hall. I had my hand pressed flat to the front-room door when, from upstairs, I heard a silly voice say: 'Would you like a marmalade sandwich, Mr Gruber?'

Kenny! That was *Kenny*. Reading from *Paddington*! My brain whirled. My fists began to clench. Kenny, my mate, pining so badly that he'd *broken in* just to come and see my sister? I yelled his name in anger and pounded up the stairs. 'Ever wondered what a cricket ball feels like when it's being whacked for six?' I screamed, and burst into Maddie's room.

They weren't there.

'We're in here,' she yelled, from Mum and Dad's room.

Mum and Dad's room? What the heck was going on? I rushed there and skidded to a halt in the doorway. Kenny was perched cross-legged on the bed, turning a page of a *Paddington* book. Maddie was sitting on a body on the floor, a man, his face pressed sideways to the carpet. He was dressed in cargo pants and scruffy white trainers and didn't look much older than a college student. His hands were tied up behind his back, secured with the cord from Mum's dressing gown. He had the gingerest hair I'd ever seen. It was falling in rasta-style knots around his neck, filling the hood of his bottle-green fleece.

'Are you the law?' he groaned, trying to lift his head. 'I ain't done no thievin'. I just wanted to take a leak.'

'Shut it,' growled Maddie, 'or I'll whack you again.' She raised her crutch. There was a dent in the handle and a bruise to match it on the ginger man's temple.

'Help me, she's mental,' he cried.

Showing no sympathy whatsoever, Maddie brought her cast down hard across his calf.

'Aw!' he yelped, making me and Kenny grimace.

'I wouldn't mess with her,' Kenny advised the bloke. 'She's in Year Nine. And she throws the discus. Lie still and listen to the story, OK? Shall I read some more now, Madz?'

Madz? Kenny was calling Maddie 'Madz'? And they'd caught a burglar? In my parents' room?

'Excuse me,' I said, banging the floor with the end of the bat, 'did I go down a rabbit hole and come out in Wonderland this morning or what? Who's *he*?!'

'White van man,' Maddie beamed proudly. 'Told you he'd been spying on us. He was going to rob us. Weren't you, carrot-face?'

'I'll have you up in court for this,' he whimpered. 'I might have brain damage.'

'No,' chirped Maddie, looping her hair, 'you'd have to be starved of *oxygen* for that.' And she bounced down on him with all her weight, squeezing every breath of air from his lungs.

'I'm ringing the police before she kills him,' I said.

'Maddie's already done it,' said Kenny. 'They should be here any—'

Appropriately, as he spoke the words, the air began to fill with wailing sirens and screeching tyres. A blue light pulsed across the ceiling as car doors slammed and feet came pounding up the stairs. First onto the landing was none other than PC Taggart. He bundled me aside and surveyed the scene. 'Blooming Nora. Is there something in the water in this house or what?'

Maddie gave him what appeared to be a look of pure lust. 'Hi, I'm Maddie, the one you didn't interrogate last time. Look, I caught a robber. I want to join the police force when I leave school. Can I put this on my application form, do you think?'

In all, six cops arrived. It was as though we were having a fancy-dress party and everyone had chosen to come in the same regulation black and white outfit. They'd arrived in force, PC Taggart explained, because the caller, the young girl (Maddie, of course), had said she was alone when the thief had broken in.

That made me feel sick to the stomach, especially when Kenny described how the door had been open when he'd turned up (hoping he could see Maddie while we were out) and how he'd heard her shouting and had run upstairs to find her struggling to hold the bloke down. All he'd done was tie the guy up, he said (with such a beguiling variety of knots that the police had to cut through the cord to cuff him). Kenny kept repeating what a star she was. But I could read the concern in PC Taggart's face. She'd been lucky. Lucky that the burglar had been physically small and not armed with a knife or high on drugs.

That was the view Mum took as well. When she arrived with Erin a few minutes later, she turned so sickly that a policewoman had to guide her into a chair. Mum refused to take anything, not even a cup of tea. All she wanted to do was hold her 'little girl'.

Eventually, Taggart prised them apart. He asked Mum's permission to ask Maddie a few questions. Looking drained, Mum nodded and went to ring Dad. As the cops took the ginger-haired bloke away and put him in the back of a police car 'for a chat', PC Taggart helped Maddie back to her room. Out came his statement sheets again. Me and Kenny piled in to listen.

'He had *no* chance,' she chirruped. 'Saw him coming from a mile off. He's been watching the house for ages. Checking us out. I s'pose he'd been waiting till he thought there was no one in. But he bungled, 'cos he wouldn't have known about me. I haven't been out since the last Ice Age, 'cos of my broken leg. So he thought he was safe to break in. Do you get it?'

PC Taggart thought he did. He rewrote it on

his sheets in 'police-speak' as he called it, reading it back for approval when he'd done: '*I had been aware for some time that a ginger-haired man who drove a white van had been loitering near the house. I looked out of my bedroom window and saw him approaching. I was concerned, because I didn't like the look of him and I was alone in the house* . . .'

'Yeah, that's cool,' Maddie said. 'Anyway, I heard the glass smash in the back door and crept out to the landing. I saw him go into the dining room first, then the front room, and then the dining room again. Are you going to check for dabs?'

'What are dabs?' asked Erin, who'd just come in with a mug of tea for Taggart.

'Fingerprints,' said Maddie, waggling her pinkies. Kenny 'waggled' back at her, making her smile. Kenny and Maddie, swapping smiles, waving. That was far scarier than someone breaking in.

PC Taggart tapped his pen against the clip of his board. 'Did you see him come out of the rooms with anything? Put anything into his pockets at all?'

'Nope,' said Maddie, shaking her head.

'How long was he in each room, can you say?'

She lifted her shoulders. 'About . . . twenty seconds each.'

Taggart frowned and sipped his tea. 'That's hardly time to nick a cushion. Has anyone checked to see if anything's out of place?'

'I went in the front room,' Erin said helpfully, 'and everything looked OK.'

'What was he after, then?' Kenny piped up.

'Car keys, I bet,' Taggart sniffed. 'That's the usual groove these days. They like to nick your keys and make off with your motor.'

'But the car wasn't here,' I pointed out.

Taggart chewed on this for a second and took another slurp of tea. 'No worries. We'll get it out of him down at the station.' He turned again to Maddie. 'What happened when he came upstairs?'

'Right,' she said eagerly, squirming on her bum to fix herself into a good position. She looped her hair and her brown eyes sparkled. She was going to enjoy this, you could tell. 'It was ace. I guessed he'd go into Mum and Dad's room first, 'cos that's the one nearest the stairs, yeah? So I crept along the landing and watched him through the crack of the door. He was looking in the wardrobes, when—'

'The wardrobes?' Taggart paused her. 'He wasn't rifling drawers?'

Maddie gave him her best disgruntled stare. 'If he was looking in drawers, I'd have said so. OK?'

Taggart scribbled on his sheet. 'Go on.' He rolled a hand.

Maddie set herself again. 'I waited till he got to the last door of Mum's wardrobe, then I sneaked up behind him and cracked him on the head with the end of my crutch. He went *urrgghhh* and fell over, grabbing at her dresses. I hope he hasn't spilled any blood on her corset; she needs that for a ball; she'll be mad if he's ruined it. Anyway, I thought about shoving him in and wedging the door shut, but there wouldn't have been room, not with all Mum's boots. So I jumped on him instead and held him down. Then Kenny came round and tied him up, dead tight. Are you writing this down or what?'

'Tom?' WPC Janesmith appeared at the door.

'What's he saying?' Taggart asked her.

The policewoman beckoned him onto the landing. They spoke in hushed tones for half a minute, before Taggart stepped back in. He ran a hand through his hair and stuck his thumb into his belt. 'Before you hit him, did he threaten you or shout abuse or anything?'

'No,' replied Maddie, 'he never got a chance.'

I looked at Janesmith. Her expression was grim. 'You're sure he didn't lunge at you or flash an arm or anything?'

'Nope,' said Maddie. 'I swatted him like a fly.'

'She would. She's really hard,' said Kenny.

'Shut up,' said Taggart, 'this is important. You were frightened of him, though? You must have been panicked?'

Dad burst in before Maddie could respond. Breathless and flushed, he went straight to her side, hugging her head to the centre of his chest.

'Dad, pack it in, I can't breathe,' she hissed. She pushed him off, embarrassed, and straightened her top.

'Do you know him?' Dad panted at the waiting police. 'This ginger-haired swine you've got in the car?'

'He's not a regular customer,' Janesmith answered quietly.

'Well, keep him away from me,' Dad bristled, his eyes full of menace and his voice choking threats.

A quick glance passed between the two coppers.

'In the circumstances, that would be advisable,' said Taggart.

My stomach took a twist. 'Why? What do you mean?'

'Well, answer him,' said Dad, as both police faltered.

WPC Janesmith took off her cap. 'He's accusing your daughter of assault,' she said.

CHAPTER TWENTY

For a moment or two the room went very quiet. Then this red-faced rage began to rise in Dad, and he was arguing with the police and they were gripping his arms and shouting in his face that he should just cool down if he didn't want to end up in the nick himself.

Nightmare.

Still, he persisted. 'She's a child. Fourteen. With a broken leg, dammit!'

'We're aware of that,' Taggart said hotly. 'And we'll do all we can to protect the girl. But right now, firing off is not going to solve things.'

'What is there to solve?' Dad hammered back. 'She was defending herself against a prowler!'

'Calm down, Mr Hadleigh,' Janesmith said, cocking an ear to her radio a second. 'We're on your side, OK? If this lad's got any kind of record he'll know how to play the system to its max. He's probably just trying it on out of spite or to get his solicitor to lever a deal.'

'Deal?' Dad spat.

'Tit for tat,' said Taggart. 'If we prosecute him

for breaking and entering, he'll push the assault charge all the way. He'll claim he had no intention of harming your daughter and that he was the one abused, if any.'

I looked at Maddie, pulling a tissue back and forth through her hands. The meniscus of a tear began to cloud one eye. 'I didn't hit him hard. You won't arrest me, will you? Dad, will I have to go to prison?' She reached out for him, but it was Kenny who immediately went to her side. To my utter amazement, she felt for his hand.

'She was scared,' he said. 'I was there. I saw it. It's a good job I came upstairs when I did, 'cos he was shouting things and swearing and stuff, saying how much he was going to hurt her and break her other leg and . . . do things to her.'

It was a lie, we all knew it (except Erin, who looked terrified), but PC Taggart clearly didn't care. 'I'm going to have a chat with this joker myself. I'll be up again shortly to complete a full statement. In the meantime' – he turned to Maddie – 'I suggest you think carefully about how you felt just prior to lashing out. As for you' – he eyeballed Kenny – 'just you be sure you get your story good and straight.' He stabbed his pen into his pocket and threw his clipboard onto the bed. 'Look after them,' he said to Janesmith. And giving Dad a nod, he swept downstairs.

Nothing happened for another three days. Dad rang the police station several times to try to find out what was going on, but all they would say was someone would come back and speak to us soon.

This was no help to Mum or Maddie. The waiting was making both of them frantic. Before leaving the house, Taggart had said that in his opinion any charges of assault would be laughed out of court. The very mention of 'court' had sent Mum into a spin. I came home from school on the Monday after the break-in and found her on the sofa, closed up like a baby. Erin, who'd been walked home by another parent because Mum refused to leave Maddie alone, had started cooking tea as if nothing was wrong. I was proud of Erin during those two days. In the past, Mum had barked at her for not doing chores. Now, in a crisis, she was holding us together.

Eventually, the dreaded visit came. They sent a detective inspector round. Detective Inspector Anthony Mellion, in plain black trousers and a casual jacket. Shoulder-length hair, thick and untidy. Eyes, by contrast, small and sharp. They were grey-blue and matched the stripes of his shirt. He settled on the leading edge of the sofa.

Mum and Dad asked me to leave the room with Erin.

'No, I'd like Joel to stay,' he said. 'I have a few questions I'd like to ask him.'

'What's Joel got to do with it?' Dad kicked in, his mercury racing up the scale again.

Mellion ignored him and turned to Erin. 'Your sister about?'

Erin shrugged and pulled a lock of loose hair into her mouth.

'Maddie's upstairs,' Mum answered for her, nervously picking at the seams of a cushion. 'Since she broke her leg, she's not wanted to come down.'

Mellion nodded and stroked his tie. 'I just thought someone might like to inform her that no charges are going to be brought against her.'

'Thank God,' Mum said and sank into a heap.

Erin stopped chewing and shot upstairs.

Dad buried his lips in Mum's hair for a second, then turned bitterly on Mellion and said, 'Took your time, didn't you, working that out?'

Unfazed, the inspector twiddled his thumbs. 'Strange as it seems, even thieves have rights. It's our duty to investigate any allegation of assault, Mr Hadleigh. Kilburn – that's your intruder's name by the way – was attacked, unprovoked, and visibly marked. Your daughter, Madeleine, wasn't. All right?'

Dad turned away, looking hurt and embarrassed.

Mellion popped a stick of gum into his mouth, folding it on his tongue before he went on. 'No one in their right mind wanted or expected your daughter to be prosecuted. But the law is the law and we had to do our job. As it happened, we quickly persuaded young Mr Kilburn that the odds were not very much in his favour. Even he could appreciate that the courts would have overwhelming sympathy for a girl of fourteen, alone in her bedroom, partially immobilized and, according to the colourful testimony of one Kenneth Jones, 'scared out of her tree'. Defence would have taken the view that if she'd given Kilburn half a chance to retaliate, who knows what he'd have done.'

Mum shuddered and said, 'I don't want to hear this.'

'No,' said Mellion, 'I can appreciate that.' He danced his toes on the rug for a second. Then in a brighter tone he announced: 'As it happens, it's not the real reason I'm here.' He tapped the sofa with his finger. 'Joel, sit down.'

Terrified, I looked at Dad. He was puzzled, like me, but nodded his consent.

Mellion moved up to let me in beside him. 'I want to take you back to the break-in a second. One of the things that baffled me most when I looked through Constable Taggart's notes was why Kilburn had spent so little time in your rooms. According to your daughter, he hopped in and out like a scalded rabbit. That left the impression he was looking for something in particular. But at the station, when we asked him to turn out his pockets, we couldn't find a thing to trace to the house. Then my eagle-eyed sergeant spotted a scrap of paper inside his shirt that he obviously didn't want us to find. This is it.'

He showed us a sealed transparent bag. Inside it was a note. All it said was:

HORACE 012

'Horace?!' I gasped.

'Not that blasted bear!' said Dad.

Mellion pulled a piece of gum off his teeth. 'When we pressed him about it, Kilburn claimed that "Horace" was a mate of his and the 012 part of a telephone number. I was suspicious, but couldn't find a reason to disbelieve him. Then, purely by chance, I suspended the interview to grab a cup of coffee and overheard our desk sergeant taking the pip out of Taggart for "arresting" a teddy bear earlier in the week. The desk sergeant gave the bear a name: Horace. So I quizzed Taggart about it and discovered that not only had he been at your house a week before, but that the bear you'd found was worth a small fortune. After that, it was obvious what Kilburn had been looking for.'

'But how did he know we had him?' I asked.

'Good question,' the inspector said. 'I couldn't make that connection either, and Kilburn was keeping his mouth tight shut. So we held him overnight while I did some digging. On a hunch, I went back and looked at the file regarding the break-in at Percy Arnold's. I checked the forensics and, lo and behold, whose prints matched those taken at the time of the Arnolds' burglary?'

'You're joking!' said Dad.

'Clear as daisies,' said Mellion. 'So then we had him. I laid into him, hard, reminding him what had happened to Mrs Arnold and threatening to throw some nasty-sounding charges at him if he didn't play ball. He played all right, Premiership stuff. Do you recognize the man in this picture?' He showed me a photo of a dark-haired, well-tanned, middle-aged man.

'It's Christopher Cholmondeley,' I said.

'Ever had any dealings with him?'

I nodded and told him what had happened at school.

Dad crooked his neck to take a better look. 'Are you saying that Kilburn was working for Cholmondeley? Stealing antique items to order?'

Mellion smiled and parted his hands. 'Two years ago, Percy Arnold took an antique brooch and some earrings to Cholmondeley for an insurance valuation. According to Kilburn, Cholmondeley picked the old man's brain about his security arrangements at home. When a suitable time had elapsed, Cholmondeley sent Kilburn to rob Mr Arnold, with specific instructions about what to steal and where he might find it. Kilburn did a nice job. Despite his shabby appearance, he knows his trade. He got the jewellery, but took a souvenir besides.'

'Horace,' said Erin, slipping back into the room.

The inspector nodded. 'Kilburn and his partner of the time had a toddler. Christmas was coming. Daddy thought the kiddie might like a free present. So he lifted your teddy bear, completely unaware that it was three times more valuable than the jewels he'd pinched. We know that Kilburn parted from this woman a few months later. We're still in the process of tracking her down, but it was she, we think, who gave the bear to the charity shop.'

'Is that how he got so damaged?' I asked. 'Because Kilburn's toddler played with him?'

'I've no idea,' said Mellion, lifting his shoulders. 'All we can assume for now is that the mother ditched the bear when it got too raggy.'

From the corner of my eye I saw Erin pout.

Mum stroked her hand as Mellion went on. 'The first Cholmondeley knew about the bear was when Joel turned up with it at school that day. He guessed right away it was worth a bit of money, made a few calls and realized how collectable it was. He quickly found your name and address and sent Kilburn out on another mission, to find the bear marked HORACE zero one two. You can imagine how Kilburn must have felt when he realized this was the bear he'd nicked before and his ex must have chucked. So he staked out your house, counted the family members and waited his moment, not realizing, of course, that your daughter was bed-bound and effectively not present. The rest you know. Should have been an easy steal for him. Instead he ends up with a lump on his head and a longish jail term, with any luck.'

'But we haven't had Horace for a week,' said Mum. 'PC Taggart took him away.'

'Yes, he's safely locked up,' said Mellion.

'In prison?' gasped a horrified Erin.

The policeman chuckled. 'In a room where we store vital evidence,' he said. 'He'll be returned to Mr Arnold shortly.'

'You still haven't explained why Kilburn thought we still had him,' said Dad.

Mellion buttoned up his jacket. 'Pure misfortune. Realistically, he couldn't watch the house every day. If he'd seen Taggart's squad car turn up last week, he would have stayed clear. Then we'd have lost him. As it is, you've helped us to break a crime wave that's been puzzling us for years.' He gathered up his notes and shook Dad's hand. 'I'm sorry it's been such a torturous few days, but thank you, anyway.'

'Our pleasure,' said Dad, though he clearly didn't mean it.

I knew that, like me, he was taking stock, summing up all the misery in his mind. Yes, we'd caught a thief – two thieves, in fact. But what were we left with in return? Dad, still faced with a mountain of debt; Mum, screwed up with nerves; Maddie, phobic, with a leg in plaster; me almost owning a criminal record; and Erin? Well, Erin was fine, just growing up faster than she might have expected.

When you looked at it like that, no good had come from my time with Horace. Not surprisingly, his name wasn't mentioned much. And so we all settled down to our gloom once more, little knowing there was one twist yet to come. That the next unexpected visitor we'd see would turn out to be our guardian angel.

His name?

The ice-cream millionaire, Percy Arnold.

CHAPTER TWENTY-ONE

He turned up the following Sunday afternoon. Erin ran to answer the doorbell and came back clutching a business card. 'Dad, there's this funny old man on the step. He says he wants to talk to us.'

She handed him the card.

'Percy Arnold?' Dad muttered.

I pulled my head from the pages of a book. Dad showed me the card. It was a smart buff colour with blue printed text. Next to the address was a drawing of a double scoop ice-cream cone.

Scratching his head, Dad went to see. A few muffled exchanges followed. I heard Mr Arnold say, 'Thank you, most kind.' And a few seconds later he appeared in the lounge, with Dad, Mum and Erin falling in behind.

'Hello, Joel,' he said. There was kindness in his voice, but all I had for him was a grunt of resentment. This was the man who'd shopped me to the cops. Why would I want to talk to him?

Mum pounded a cushion. 'Sit here, Mr Arnold.' She gestured to an armchair. 'Cup of tea?'

'Oh, please don't go to any trouble, Mrs Hadleigh.'

'It's no trouble,' said Mum, giving Erin a nudge.

Erin did her slave frown and hurried to the kitchen, leaving Mr Arnold's stick in a corner.

Percy hitched up his trousers and eased himself down, crossing his legs with an elegant sweep. He'd come dressed in what Gran would call his 'Sunday best': a dark blue suit, white collar, smart tie. No morsels of food round his mouth today.

'You must be quite surprised to see me,' he said. 'After all that's happened, I expect I must be one of the last people you'd wish to have visit you on a Sunday afternoon. So I'll be brief.' He smiled at Mum, then levelled his pale blue gaze at me. 'I've come to set the record straight. I'd like to apologize to Joel, here, for ringing the local police when I did, and for putting the family through what must have been some trying moments.'

Dad massaged his lips and didn't reply. It was Mum, pressing a thumb into her palm, who said, 'We all understand why you did it, Mr Arnold. We know you've had some difficult moments yourself.' She was careful not to make any mention of his wife, but the ghost of her was dancing between the words.

Mr Arnold steepled his fingers. 'You're very kind, Mrs Hadleigh, but I don't think you do – understand, I mean. You see, when Joel brought Horace – as you call him – to me, I knew right away he was being untruthful about how long he'd been in possession of the bear. I believe if I'd challenged him there, on the spot, he would have told me everything and all this unpleasantness could have been avoided. Am I right, Joel?'

My cheeks reddened. Erin backed in with a tea tray and biscuits, sparing me the need to make a confession. Mum hurriedly cleared a space on the coffee table as Mr Arnold carried on talking.

'I can't truthfully explain why I didn't give Joel the chance to own up. Anger, I suppose, clouding my judgement. I still think every day about Florence and what happened to her when that boy broke in. She was in the house, you know. He pushed her aside as he made his escape. She saw him take the bear and begged him to leave it. It had been her treasured friend since childhood. She was younger than your daughter . . .'

'Erin,' said Erin, as he fished for her name.

'Charming,' he said with a grandfatherly smile. '. . . than Erin here, when it was given to her.'

'That's dreadful,' said Mum. 'She must have been devastated.'

'She was,' he replied, his freckled head bowing forward a little.

Erin quickly revived his spirits. 'What is Horace's proper name?'

'Ah.' Mr Arnold struck the air with his finger. 'Frederick – or Freddie, which was also the name of my wife's father. But I rather like Horace, don't you?'

'I like them both,' said Erin, in a voice that ranged between posh and Victorian. With one finger on the lid of the teapot, she poured. 'It was horrible, what happened to Freddie. I'm glad you got him back. I wish that *I* had a bear like him.'

That seemed to touch Mr Arnold deeply. He leaned forward and patted Erin gently on the elbow. 'Thank you. It means a great deal to me to see him again. Which brings me neatly to this.' From his inside pocket, he took out a cheque book.

'What's this?' said Dad, looking bewildered.

Mr Arnold unscrewed a fountain pen. 'The police have given me a detailed account of what took place here the other day. I was quite mortified to hear about the fracas between your elder daughter and the young villain who broke in. She is all right, I trust?'

'Erin, who was that at the door?' yelled Maddie. Big gob. Right on cue, as usual.

'That's her. And yes, she's all right,' Dad drawled. 'Erin, go up and see to her, will you?'

Erin shook her head. It wasn't every day you saw a millionaire's cheque book. Like me, she was watching Mr Arnold closely. My nerves began to jangle like a windchime as he said, 'I had quite a chat with Inspector Mellion, the officer who's taken charge of the case. He informed me, Joel, that your intention was to seek out the original owner of the bear. Is that correct?'

I looked at Mum, who encouraged me to explain. 'I thought if he was worth a lot of money then the person who'd put him in the shop ought to know.'

Mr Arnold nodded. In a slow and steady hand, he began to date the cheque. 'Well, I'm afraid the inspector didn't believe you. But that's the lot of a policeman, I suppose: to question facts and have suspicions. I, on the other hand, *do* believe you. And this is my way of proving it.' The pen looped and scratched across the book. 'After Florence died, I offered a reward for information leading to the arrest of the thief, or for the safe return of the bear. He was insured, of course, to his full value, but I always refused to make a claim, hoping that he might one day be found. Now he has and the reward still stands. As far as I'm concerned, it belongs to you.' He finished on his signature and boldly underlined it.

'A reward?' gasped Erin. Her eyes took on that Christmas Day look.

Mum turned to Dad. 'Trevor?' she queried, meaning 'What are you going to do?'

Dad blustered. 'Mr Arnold, we—'

'I won't hear a word of refusal, Mr Hadleigh, no matter how noble or well-intentioned. The facts of the matter are plain: Joel rescued the bear and through kindness preserved him.' He flapped the cheque in the air to dry the ink. 'I've made this out to your father, Joel, because I hope the whole family will benefit from it. But I'd like you to see it first.'

He handed me the cheque. I read it and wobbled. Dad turned his face away as he handed it on to Mum. 'We can't accept that,' he said.

'You can, and you will,' Mr Arnold said bluntly, screwing the top onto his fountain pen in the manner of a man who'd secured a lot of deals.

'Show me,' said Erin, bobbing up and down

and eating her hair. She leaned across Mum. *'Five thousand pounds?!'*

Mr Arnold smiled, as if all he'd done was pop a donation into someone's tin.

I looked at Mum again. A backlog of unshed tears were lighting her dark eyes, making them shine. 'Mr Arnold,' she began, 'we really don't deserve—' The creak of the living-room door made her pause.

Maddie was standing in the doorway, looking on. 'What?' she said to our gawping faces, as if she'd merely nipped out to the kitchen for a biscuit.

'Oh, Maddie,' Mum sniffed. 'Oh, my brave little girl.' She stood up and ran to her, squeezing her so hard that Maddie had to let her crutches go loose. They fell away along with three weeks of suffering.

'That's Maddie,' said Erin, meeting Mr Arnold's blue-eyed gaze. 'She doesn't come down very often these days.' She returned to the tea things and held up a spoon. 'Would you like one lump of sugar or two?'

CHAPTER TWENTY-TWO

No one asked Maddie for an explanation. No one made a fuss. No one else cried. Dad helped her into the big armchair and used a leather footstool to support her cast. 'OK?' he asked, giving her toes a celebratory wiggle.

She nodded and looped her nut-brown hair. She was wearing her fluffy light-blue dressing gown. Underneath it I could see her *Stargirl* T-shirt. She was making an effort. Coming back. That moment, more than any other that day, made me feel certain we were going to be all right.

'Are you the ice-cream bloke?' she asked.

'Oh, Maddie, really!' Mum's scowl burned the tears off her face in an instant. It was funny to see Mum huffing again. Funny and . . . I tightened my lip and felt a lump come to my throat.

Mr Arnold, stout as ever, replied, 'I am the man responsible for Percy's ices. Why, do you like them?'

Maddie planed a hand. 'I like the stuff you get at the pictures better.'

'Madd-*ie.*' Now it was Dad's turn to chew a little grit. 'Don't believe her, Mr Arnold. This family's been more than grateful for your ice-cream production down the years.'

Percy Arnold stirred his tea and took a bourbon biscuit. 'Yes, it's been a strange vocation. Who would have thought that empires could be built on flavoured milk? And you, Mr Hadleigh? What's your profession?'

Dad stretched the reward cheque between his fingers. 'I run my own business, cleaning carpets.'

The drag in his voice was painfully clear. Mr Arnold wasn't slow to pick up on it. 'Not through choice, by the sound of things?'

Dad wet his lips and tried to sound positive. 'I lost a big client recently, a very lucrative contract. I'm not sure we deserve your reward, but I won't pretend that it won't help to stem a few problems.'

'Reward?' asked Maddie.

Erin whispered the amount.

Maddie's jaw sprang open. 'Cool! Does that mean I can go riding again when this thing's off?'

'Madd-*ie!*' Now it was Erin's turn to chide her.

Mr Arnold laughed as the girls did a little tongue-poking. 'And how about you, Mrs Hadleigh? Are you involved with carpets as well?'

'Oh, no,' she laughed, 'except to print invoices and keep the books tidy. I have enough of a job looking after these four.'

'Mum sews,' said Erin. 'She makes costumes. She's clever. She was going to mend Horace – I mean, Freddie – but Joel wouldn't let her, 'cos he wanted to draw him all messed up.'

Mr Arnold put his tea cup into his saucer. 'Yes, Freddie will require some careful attention if he's to be restored to his former glory. You'd be up to that task, then, would you, Mrs Hadleigh?'

Mum's big brown eyes grew round with indecision. 'Oh, I'm not sure. At the time I offered to stitch him back together we thought he was only worth fifty pence. There's a world of difference between mending a raggy old teddy and a valuable antique. I'd hate to bodge it.'

'You wouldn't,' said Erin, as if to think so was unthinkable. She snatched up a large, embroidered cushion and thrust it under Mr Arnold's nose. 'Mum did this.'

'Very accomplished,' he muttered, putting on a pair of half-moon specs as he struggled to focus on the fine needlework.

'Get the portfolio,' Maddie said to Erin.

Erin shot across the room and dragged a large black folder from between a bookcase and the window wall.

'Girls . . .' Mum tutted.

Dad shook his head and laughed. 'Now you've done it. Showtime, Mr Arnold. Tell us when it gets too much.'

Erin dropped to her knees and unzipped the folder. From it fell a muddled heap of patterns and sketches. 'These are pictures and drawings of all the different costumes and things Mum's made.'

'Quite a collection,' Mr Arnold said, as Erin turned the papers and Maddie explained what each was about.

'That's a Captain Hook coat she did for this author bloke. And that's a ball gown she made and the corset that goes with it; it's dead pretty and it hides her bouncy castle—'

'Her what?' I asked.

'Her middle-age spread.'

'MADDIE?!' Mum shrieked, glowing like a stop sign.

'Oh, oh, and that's a kangaroo suit she made for a party! *That* was furry. *That's* sort of bear-like.'

'It's nothing at all like a bear!' Mum huffed. She grabbed the portfolio and snapped it shut. 'Mr Arnold, you're very kind to enquire about my skills, but mending Horace would be a job for a specialist, not a simple hobbyist like me.'

Mr Arnold removed his glasses again and

packed them away in a solid grey case. 'I agree some guidance would be required – as well as the correct tools and materials, naturally. But from what I've seen here, that wouldn't be beyond you. Margarete Steiff, the founder of the famous Steiff Bear company, began her career as a dressmaker, too. And I'm sure Mr Lucan would be willing to help.'

'Mr Lucan?'

'The man at the bear shop,' I said.

'And, of course, he'd need cleaning,' Mr Arnold went on.

Dad stirred to a start, realizing this comment was aimed at him. 'Not with anything industrial,' he said, narrowing his eyes in professional mode. 'Soap suds and a cotton wool bud is all I'd want to risk on something that old. I bet it would take for ever, too.'

'I've waited two years,' Mr Arnold said tenderly. 'I think I could wait a few more weeks.'

'Oh, Mum, do it,' Erin begged, swinging on the arm of the chair like a chimp. 'Please, I'll help you. I promise. Oh, please.'

'Naturally, there would be a fee,' said Percy. 'I could hardly expect you to labour for nothing.'

'Mum, don't be a wuss. Just go for it,' said Maddie.

'I'll "wuss" you, cheeky.' They exchanged a slapped palm.

Mum looked at us all in turn. 'Why do I feel like I'm being press-ganged? Mr Arnold, it's a thirty-thousand-pound liability!'

Percy Arnold didn't speak. He seemed more concerned with the texture of the biscuit he was dunking in his tea.

Mum threw up her hands. 'All right, I'll have a go.'

'Yes!' went Erin, knocking her fists.

Mum smiled and gave her a cuddle. 'As it happens, my mother had a bear like Horace. I watched her mend a joint or two. I *think* – with a little professional help – I can do it. I'll take on the task of cleaning him, too; Trevor won't have the patience for that. But' – she paused to point a 'naughty boy' finger at Percy – 'I do not want a single penny in return. You've already given us a sizeable reward. I'll do this out of kindness – and as compensation for all the trouble that Joel has caused.'

'Mum?!' I protested.

Both girls sniggered.

'Excellent. I agree,' Mr Arnold said, clapping his hands down flat to his thighs. 'I'll have Freddie—' He paused to take a word from Erin.

'Horace,' she said, 'while he's here.'

'Quite right. I'll have Horace brought round to you first thing tomorrow.' He smiled at us all. 'Well, this has been most enjoyable. I look forward to doing business with you, Mrs Hadleigh. Thank you for listening to my side of the story. And for the biscuits. And the tea, Erin.' She blushed and looked away. 'Joel, pass me my stick, if you would.'

I fetched it gladly and helped him to his feet.

'Thank you,' he said, and gave my arm a squeeze.

And I knew with that one touch that he'd forgiven me, completely, and all would be well.

Mr Arnold was happy.

My family was happy.

And Horace was coming back.

CHAPTER TWENTY-THREE

The only thing that wasn't right was me and Roopindar. As life began to settle back to normal again, it seemed so unfair that we should be kept apart from one another. Word of what had happened had reached her via Laura, who'd been picking Kenny's brain since the day of our break-up. And every now and then a reply would come back.

Roo's really pleased that Horace is OK. She misses you loads, but there's nothing she can do. She says please don't look at her in the classroom. It hurts. You have to forget her. Please.

Every day it got to me a little bit more.

It came to a peak on the Friday before half term, when I knew I wouldn't see her for at least a week. It was a sunny afternoon, baking hot. I was out in the garden with Kenny and the girls, drawing angels all over Maddie's cast. She'd decided at last that she wanted souvenirs (like pieces of 'wedding cake') to take into school once the cast came off. I had been commissioned to make the bits look 'collectable'. Erin, on the other side of Maddie's raised leg, was colouring in the angels I'd already drawn. Kenny was sitting at Maddie's feet. All three of them were playing this ridiculous game about who knew the stupidest or most bizarre fact.

'OK, I know one,' Maddie chirped eagerly. 'I read this in a magazine: giraffes can clean their ears with their tongues.'

A blade of grass tilted off Kenny's lip. 'No way.'

'Their *ears*?' Erin queried, from under the brim of her white floppy hat. She pushed her tongue beyond the sides of her mouth in a vain attempt to lick her lobes.

Maddie lifted her jet-black shades and said, 'Excuse me, you're not a giraffe, OK?'

'Stop fidgeting,' I tutted, without looking up. Every time Maddie made the slightest move my pencil would jump like a lie detector needle. (So what did she do? Pull her top down off her shoulders to catch the sun.)

'OK, I believe it,' Erin peeped. 'They eat leaves off tall trees; they've got to reach them somehow.'

'That's what their necks are for: *reaching*,' said Kenny. 'Only aliens could clean their ears with their tongues.'

'Vote,' said Maddie. 'All those who believe it?' She and Erin raised their hands. 'Joel, come on.'

'I'm drawing. Do you want these angels or not?'

'Oh, listen to Mr Grumpy, *again*. Every day this week: whinge, whinge, whinge. Chill out, will you? Come on, vote.'

I sighed. I believed it. I raised my hand.

'There, I win,' Maddie said, smirking. She aimed a pimple of tongue at Kenny.

'I know a better one, though,' he said. 'Bet you didn't know that leeches have got thirty-two brains.'

Maddie screwed up her nose and said with a snort, 'Oh yeah, like we'd really believe *that*. Like someone really took the trouble to count them.'

'It's true. We learned it in biology, didn't we, Joel?'

'Can't remember,' I muttered, haloing an angel. 'Maddie, sit *still*.'

'Why do they need thirty-two?' asked Erin. 'I mean, what do leeches think about?'

'Leeching!' Kenny and Maddie hooted.

I pulled back, counting, gritting my teeth. One more chance, that's all she'd get.

'Vote,' Maddie called, as Mum came up behind her and started massaging her bare white shoulders.

'You should be wearing your sun block, madam. Iced tea, anyone? Vote on what?'

'Leeches,' said Erin. She asked Mum's opinion about the brains.

'Ooh, I don't know,' was Mum's reply. 'Seems a bit unfair to goldfish, does that.'

'Goldfish?' Maddie's perplexed look spoke for us all.

'Hmm. Goldfish can't have much of a brain, because their memory-span is only seven seconds.'

'How do you know?' asked Kenny.

'*Well*,' said Mum, using gravity to bottom out the word. 'If you listen closely while they're swimming round their bowls you'll hear them gurgle, "Ooh, look, a sunken castle," whenever they go past it – every seven seconds, on average.'

Maddie squealed with high-pitched laughter. 'Mum, you're mental. You're worse than him.' She jabbed her foot at Kenny, who slid a blade of grass between her toes, making her squeal even louder than before.

That was it. I threw down my pencil and marched.

I heard Maddie moan, 'What is *wrong* with him?'

Then Mum, hurrying after me: 'Joel, what's the matter?' She stopped me near the kitchen and turned me round. 'Hey, what is it?'

'Nothing. It's just . . . them.'

'Who?'

'*Them*. I was s'posed to be drawing. If they want to act soppy, why don't they just go to the park or something?'

Mum folded her arms in that deliberately slow manner that parents use when they think they know they're on to something. 'This isn't about Kenny and Maddie, is it?'

'Who else would I mean?'

She tilted her head, trying to make eye contact. 'Roopindar, perhaps?'

'I'm going in,' I muttered, and broke away before she could speak again. That was the trouble with parents sometimes. They were just too good at guessing the truth . . .

. . . they were also good at passing it on.

That same night, without any warning, Dad put me in the car and drove me to Roopindar's.

My heart rate doubled when I saw where we were stopping. 'Dad, what are we doing?'

He killed the engine and opened his door. 'I had a chat with Roopindar's dad this afternoon.'

'What about?'

'What do you think? You want to see her again, don't you?'

'But—?'

'No promises. Just be polite and listen patiently to what Mr Seehra has to say. Come on, or we're going to be late.'

Roo's mother let us in and took us straight into the lounge, where Roopindar and her dad were waiting. Roo was sitting on the end of the sofa. Dressed in a bright green and yellow sari, she looked pretty, like a present done up for Christmas. Mr Seehra stood up to shake hands. We said hello quietly and he showed Dad to a chair. I was allowed to sit on the sofa, one cushion away from Roo. On the table were the usual bowls of nuts. Dad and I were invited to dip. Roopindar sat motionless, hands in her lap. Then the talking began.

Tipping forward in his seat, Mr Seehra spread his hands. 'Joel, your father and I talked at some length on the telephone today. He has informed me of everything that took place from the time the police came to speak with you and what happened when the ice-cream fellow, Mr Arnold, came to see you.'

I nodded (politely). Roopindar bit her lip.

'You know, I was very alarmed to learn that my daughter might have been involved in criminal activities. I thought you had led her astray, and that upset me, because I liked you a good deal. You always seemed to me to be an honourable young man, and that is something we Sikhs value highly.'

I looked at Dad. His smile, though thin, was kind and supportive. He levelled his palm in an upward gesture, meaning I should raise my head.

Mr Seehra spoke again. 'You can understand, I think, why I had to take my daughter away from you? For a girl like Roopindar to be accused of stealing is terribly shameful to all her family. At the time, I had to act upon what I knew and be sure that no more disgrace would follow. But that was then, and this is now.' He shifted in his seat. The green leather groaned. 'I was impressed that your father chose to speak to me today. It proved to me how much he cares about his son and that made me sympathetic to what he had to say. I thought a great deal about his words; and when I had thought, I prayed for a while; and when I had prayed, I saw things clearly. I realized your actions were admittedly misguided and not the kind of behaviour I would find acceptable for my daughter to be a part of, but I did understand that your intentions were good. I myself heard you say that you wished to seek out the true owner of the bear. By a strange means you have done that, and in my heart I applaud you for it.' He stroked his beard and looked me up and down. 'So, here are the words I expect you'd like to hear. I would be a very poor father and an equally bad Sikh if I did not listen to any kind of plea which aimed to resolve another person's suffering. Therefore, I am removing this curfew between you and my daughter, always remembering: no shenanigans.'

I glanced at Roo. She smiled back nervously. Mates again. Joy. Thank you, Dads.

Mr Seehra leaned forward and offered mine the nut bowl. 'Now that this awkward matter is resolved, I must ask you, Mr Hadleigh, about your business. Roopindar has told me that you've experienced some problems lately?'

'*Da-ad!*' moaned Roo. 'I told you that in private.'

'I am merely seeking to help,' he replied.

'How could you possibly help?' asked Dad.

'He's my dad,' said Roo. 'He's a genius with money.'

Her father wagged a finger. She sat back meekly.

Mr Seehra swallowed some *mattar*. 'I am an accountant; I specialize in small businesses like yours.'

'I already have an accountant,' said Dad.

Mr Seehra smiled. 'Then any advice I have to offer will be totally free of charge, will it not?'

The pair of them laughed and they began to talk.

And talk. And talk. And talk. And talk.

An hour later, Roo and I were sitting on the jetty at the bottom of the garden, when Dad called to say we were finally going home.

She let go of my arm as we walked up the lawn. She knew better than to push it, in front of her father. Running to him she said, 'Joel has invited me to tea, Daddy-ji. On Sunday. May I go? It's a special occasion.'

Mr Seehra thrust his hands into his pockets. It made him look like a pear-drop beside her. 'Is Sunday your birthday, Joel?'

I shook my head. 'No. Mr Arnold's coming round – for Horace.'

CHAPTER TWENTY-FOUR

He looked fantastic. Horace, that is. Mum had spent hours every day with him, lovingly cleaning each patch of fur like an archaeologist uncovering a long-lost tomb. For three weeks she hadn't let anyone near him, claiming that the impact would be so much more impressive if we saw the change in him all at once.

She was right. We were gobsmacked. Even Maddie let out a gasp of awe when Mum unveiled the 'new' Horace to us. His fur was pure honey, soft enough to make your fingers tingle, so bright it appeared to be permanently sunlit.

Erin went wild. 'Can I hold him?' she begged. 'Oh, can I? Oh, please?'

'No, he stays on the table,' said Mum, putting Horace down and preening a sprutty bit of fur on his snout. 'I don't want him ruffled at this late stage.'

'He's so cute,' said Roo, looking over Erin's shoulder. 'Did he always have a bow?'

Mum shook her head. 'Special, twenty-first-century addition.' She adjusted the ribbon round Horace's neck. I thought it looked tacky, a blue satin bow, but Mr Arnold would probably appreciate the sentiment.

From his stool in the corner, Kenny said, 'Bet it's worth tons of money now.'

'Honestly, is that all you ever think about?' Maddie, perched like a parrot on the end of Kenny's knee, gave his foot a nudge with her heel.

There was a pause, then Kenny answered: 'I think about football. And homework. And you.'

'Aaah,' went Roopindar, looking as if she'd like to be a bridesmaid at their wedding.

To everyone's relief, the doorbell rang before Kenny could propose.

'I'll get it,' Dad shouted from down the hall.

Then it was demented bees time in the kitchen as we all bumped around rearranging ourselves. Mum plumped her hair as if the Queen was coming, Erin moved in front of Horace so he couldn't be seen and I leaned back against the worktop with Roo.

In came Mr Arnold, suited again, followed by Dad, carrying a large tub of ice-cream. 'Treat,' he announced.

Maddie strained to see past the blockage that was Erin.

'*Percy's* chocolate ripple,' I told her.

'None of your cinema stuff, this,' Dad quipped. 'Shall I put it in the freezer?'

'Certainly not,' said Mum, fluttering like a girl as Mr Arnold kissed her hand. 'Dishes, Erin.'

Erin shook her head. This was her moment and she wasn't going to waste it. 'Mr Arnold, look over here,' she gushed, and stepped away from the kitchen table.

The room fell into absolute silence. For a moment, Mr Arnold simply turned his head and stared at Horace in stunned amazement. Maddie, craning forward, nearly slipped off Kenny's knee as we waited, breathlessly, for the old man's reaction. Then, as if the sun had risen inside him, his eyes began to shine and he moved towards the table. His aged hands trembled as he picked up his bear and held him as though they were going to waltz, one palm under him, one at his back.

'Magnificent,' he whispered. 'Simply magnificent.'

Dad found Mum's shoulders and gave them a squeeze. 'Not bad, is she, Mr Arnold?'

'Are you happy with him? Really happy?' asked Mum.

'Words fail me,' Mr Arnold said, letting his blue eyes rise and fall, taking in the ears and the newly-stitched pads. He moved the sewn limb up and down, leaving it set like one of those old-fashioned railway signals. He chuckled quietly and rustled the bow. 'I never saw him, you realize, when he was new. Florence was twenty-eight when we were married. She'd already had him for many years. She would be very proud now.'

That did it for Mum. Big tissue moment. In my heart, I was reaching for the box myself. This was it, the pinnacle of everything I'd been through. I had found Horace's rightful owner and now was the time for me to give him back. I suppose I should have felt all 'good and virtuous' as Mr Grace was always praying for his pupils to be. But the truth was, a small chasm of despair had opened up in my chest and I didn't know how to stop it growing. Horace was going. I didn't want to lose him, but how could I keep him? I saw Mr Arnold cast a glance my way. I swallowed hard and stared at the pattern in the floor tiles. I was on the precipice of tears when Erin came to my rescue.

'What's that?' she asked. She was pointing to a small old-fashioned trunk, with worn leather straps and tarnished buckles. Mr Arnold had left it just inside the hall.

'That's a carrier,' he announced, easing down into a chair. 'Could someone bring it in?'

Dad hoisted it onto the table. 'It's not very heavy. What's in it, Mr Arnold?'

'Nothing,' guessed Maddie, standing up now for a better view (Kenny rubbed his knee and sighed with relief). 'That's what he's taking Horace home in.'

'Oh, yes,' said Erin, becoming still.

'Let's find those dishes,' Mum said quietly. Roo immediately offered her assistance. I turned away, too, to serve up the ice-cream. I couldn't bear to see Horace sealed up in a case, to be taken away like a ventriloquist's dummy.

'Can I open it?' said Kenny.

'Please do,' said Mr Arnold.

Kenny pulled the straps. The buckles rattled. *Traitor*, I was thinking, digging deep into the ice-cream. *I hope you get a toenail. I hope you—*

'Another one?' he grunted.

Roo and I turned like a pair of swing doors.

Sitting in the carrier was another bear. It was as old as Horace, possibly older, but darker and dumpier, with a pointier snout.

'Who's he?' asked Erin, eyes widening with delight.

'Theodore Albert,' Mr Arnold said proudly. 'He's my oldest and my favourite. What do you think, hmm?'

Kenny leaned closer, twitching his nose. 'He smells a bit pongy.'

'You can talk, *Voodoo Warrior*,' jeered Maddie. Even now, she hadn't forgiven Kenny for wearing what she called 'that noxious after-shave'.

'Eighty years of accumulated dust,' said Mr Arnold. 'He needs a good spruce. Wouldn't you say so, Mrs Hadleigh?'

Mum put a finger on Theodore's chest. 'I certainly wouldn't like to pat him too hard. The dust cloud would probably set off my asthma.'

'Why have you brought him here?' asked Erin.

Mr Arnold fitted his hands together as though he'd just caught a slow-moving fly. 'Call me presumptuous, but I guessed your mother would do a first-class job with Horace; I was hoping she'd repeat the magic with Theo.'

'What's his price tag, first?' Mum said quickly, before anyone else could even draw breath.

Mr Arnold plucked a spot of fluff off Theo's paw. 'He's a Merryforth, not quite as rare as Horace, and therefore worth a little less.'

That didn't do much to melt Mum's expression. If she'd scowled any darker the neighbourhood would think we'd had an eclipse. I knew what she was thinking: what's 'a little' in a millionaire's terms? A thousand? Five thousand? Ten thousand pounds?

Before she could comment, Mr Arnold spoke again. 'As it happens, I have a rather large crew of old bears in my study, all of them requiring some degree of attention. What do you say, Mrs

205

Hadleigh? Could I tempt you to become a full-time restorer?'

That seemed to set everyone talking at once. After several calls for quiet, Dad's voice climbed to the top of the pile. 'Mr Arnold, I don't mean to sound too mercenary about this, but Emma must have spent the best part of sixty hours working on Horace. Even at a minimum wage, the bill for him alone would be quite substantial – if we were charging you for him, which we're not.'

'Oh, yes, that reminds me,' the old man said. He fished in his pocket and handed Dad a small grey business card.

'Marling's? The computer firm? What's this about?'

'I play bridge with their company director. Over dinner last week we started to talk about their office cleaning budget. Naturally, I mentioned your name. He, Alan Marling, would like you to call him.'

Dad blinked and shook his head. 'Marling's? They're enormous.'

Mr Arnold smiled. 'How's that ice-cream doing?'

'Nearly there,' said Roo, licking some off her finger.

'Splendid, splendid. Now, where were we?'

'Bears,' said Erin, pointing at Theo.

I glanced at Mum, who was busily engaged in a lip-reading conversation with Dad. As he turned away flapping the Marling's card, Mr Arnold touched her sleeve and said, 'Here are my terms, Mrs Hadleigh: if you clean and repair my entire collection, I will pay you ten pounds per hour and provide all necessary tools and materials. There, what do you say?'

'Ten pounds? Every *hour*?' Maddie almost gagged.

'Maybe twelve,' said Percy, jiggling a hand. '*Twelve?*'

'Twelve fifty. That's my final offer.'

Maddie opened her mouth so wide you could have juggled all forty-nine lottery balls in it.

'But if Mum worked for sixty hours on Horace . . .' Erin tried to do the sum on her fingers.

'She'd be invoicing you for seven hundred and fifty pounds,' said Dad, looking distantly out at the garden.

'Just for cleaning one smelly *teddy*?' asked Kenny.

Mr Arnold ran a finger down Theo's ear. 'Take your time, Mrs Hadleigh. But do think about it. Please.'

Mum fanned her face and made a sort of gentle whimpering sound, as if she'd temporarily forgotten how to breathe.

'Now then, before we eat,' said Percy. 'I do have one last thing to say.' From the Aladdin's cave of his jacket, he pulled out a piece of crinkled paper. Time had yellowed its outer edges and pricked a few slits in its creases and folds. He laid it, still folded, on the table beside him, moving it in circles like a card magician. 'You'll have gathered by now that I am what most people would describe as a slightly eccentric old man. Collecting bears has been my hobby ever since I've had the means to buy them. But as the years have caught up with me, I've been facing a rather difficult dilemma: what to do with my collection when I die.'

'Oh, Mr Arnold, you mustn't think like that.'

'Oh, but I must,' he said, smiling. 'You see, Mrs Hadleigh, I have very little family, and those who do stand to inherit from me sadly don't share my love of bears.'

'Why don't you just sell them?' Kenny suggested.

'Goodness, no.' Mr Arnold shrivelled at the thought. 'I have all the money one man could ever need. Besides, Florence would never have approved. No, no. Selling them is out of the question.' His pale blue gaze came to rest on me. 'So what I've decided to do instead is *give* them away, to people who I'm certain will care for them, as I have, as Florence once did, as you have done, Joel.'

'Oh, goodness,' Mum gasped.

Erin raised her fists in hope.

Mr Arnold pushed the paper across the table, lodging it underneath Mum's fingers. 'That's a purchase and registration document. It will guarantee Horace's authenticity for valuation and insurance purposes.' He raised his hand before Dad could speak. 'Which I promise to cover now, and in the terms of my will. It's for the family, Mr Hadleigh. Please don't refuse him. It would mean so much to me if you took him.'

At the back of the room someone stifled a tear. Maddie, of all people. That was a first. Kenny hesitated once, then slipped an arm around her. As if the soppiness was catching, Roo touched my hand.

Mr Arnold tightened Horace's bow, then picked him up like a football trophy. 'You told me once you'd like to keep him. Is that still true, Joel?'

I nodded. I couldn't open my mouth.

Mr Arnold smiled and turned him round. 'Look into his eyes. Deep into his eyes. Don't be afraid. What do you see in his stare?'

I looked into the perfect, glassy orange eyes. The stare was strong and happy and proud. But it was more what I couldn't see than anything

I could. 'He doesn't look homesick any more,' I said.

'I agree,' said Mr Arnold, handing him over. He teased out the famous trademark ears. 'Not in the least bit homesick. Home.'

ABOUT THE AUTHOR

Children sometimes ask, 'Chris, how long have you been writing books?' Well, I've been *writing* since the age of thirty-two, but my first children's book wasn't published until I was thirty-nine. *Horace* will coincide with the tenth anniversary of me writing children's fiction. Good fun it's been too. In that time I will have published twenty-one books. Hopefully, there will be a lot more to come.

I've always liked bears, so it will come as no surprise to you to know that *Horace* is based on a true story. I walked into a charity shop once and saw an old bear with a 50p label on his chest. I couldn't believe they were selling such a proud bear so cheaply. So I bought him. He looked a bit threadbare – so I called him 'Fredbear' (hah!) and then Fred for short. In the book, I changed his name to protect the inno-cent. Originally, the bear Joel finds was going to be called Horatio (after Horatio Hornblower, which I was watching on TV at the time). But Horatio was a bit of a mouthful and my wife,

Jay, suggested Horace. Suits him, don't you think?